THE DAY OF THE MONSTER PIGEONS

FREEKHAM HIGH SCHOOL

STEVE COLE

OXFORD
UNIVERSITY PRESS

OXFORD
UNIVERSITY PRESS

Great Clarendon Street, Oxford OX2 6DP

Oxford University Press is a department of the University of Oxford.
It furthers the University's objective of excellence in research, scholarship,
and education by publishing worldwide in

Oxford New York

Auckland Cape Town Dar es Salaam Hong Kong Karachi
Kuala Lumpur Madrid Melbourne Mexico City Nairobi
New Delhi Shanghai Taipei Toronto

With offices in

Argentina Austria Brazil Chile Czech Republic France Greece
Guatemala Hungary Italy Japan Poland Portugal Singapore
South Korea Switzerland Thailand Turkey Ukraine Vietnam

Oxford is a registered trade mark of Oxford University Press
in the UK and in certain other countries

British Library Cataloguing in Publication Data

Data available

ISBN: 978-0-19-279276-1

1 3 5 7 9 10 8 6 4 2

Printed in Great Britain

For Sean O'Meara, who remembered

Registration

'The end of term!' Sam Innocent declared as he strolled up the school drive. 'Almost time to say, "Bye-bye, Freekham High"!'

'One whole day to get through first,' sighed Sara Knot, walking along beside him. 'And *what* a day.'

Sam paused for a moment to take in the view of the school from the top of the school drive. In a word: ugly. Modern boxy buildings lay scattered about like bricks from a giant's play-set, linked by dull concrete walkways. He switched his gaze to Sara instead, who was far easier on the eye. Tall and slim, with blonde hair down to her waist and legs up to her armpits, over the last five weeks she had become a friend, a partner-in-crime—and a fellow survivor.

Freekham High proudly proclaimed itself to be a progressive school, but in Sam and Sara's book it was just plain freaky.

1

They had both started there on the same day in May in a shower of unlikely coincidences. It turned out that each had been born at the same time on the same day—February 29th—and each had spent the last eight years attending two or three different schools each year as a result of their parents' ever-shifting jobs.

That first day at Freekham, severed thumbs started showing up all over the school . . . and Sam and Sara had found themselves caught up in several mad mysteries since then.

Now, on the last day of term, Sam actually felt a pang of regret that it was all coming to an end. Freekham High could freak you out—it was, after all, a place where weird stuff went to happen—but at least school-life was rarely dull. He and Sara had made some good friends here.

It seemed a shame that, after today, he would probably never see any of them again.

Sara nudged him. 'Are you going to stand here staring at the school all day, or would you like to get your bum in gear?'

'What sort of gear did you have in mind?' Sam enquired. 'I should say now, lacy knickers don't really suit me.'

She rolled her eyes, something she did very well—he supposed he'd given her enough practice over the last few weeks. *You'll miss me when I'm gone*, he wanted to say. Last night, his dad announced that he had almost certainly got another job, miles away. The Innocent family would be moving on once more. Another friendless summer loomed ahead for him, followed by a lonely autumn term at yet another school.

And it would all be so . . . normal.

So totally dull!

Sara was frowning at him. 'You OK?'

'Uh-huh.' He roused himself. 'Course I am. I . . . I was just watching out for another pigeon attack, that's all.'

'Should get inside, then. Out here, you're a sitting duck.'

'That's OK, then—pigeons and ducks are on the same side, aren't they? Birds of a feather stick together.'

Sara grimaced. 'Those flying rats will make you sticky, all right.'

It was a typical Freekham High phenomenon. Just lately, a flock of particularly unpleasant pigeons had been making their presence felt. It was as if they had a grudge against the school—divebombing windows, pooing on the teachers' cars . . . For some reason they had a particular fascination with Sam and Sara's form room, and had left messy presents all over the windows five times this week.

'Well, *I'm* going to the form room even if you're not,' Sara announced. 'Fido wants to run through some of my lines for the play.' She glanced up at the sky. 'Weather seems to be holding off. I only hope those pigeons do!'

Sam nodded. It wasn't only *his* last day at Freekham. Mr 'Killer' Collier, the ancient, grumpy Geography teacher was finally retiring after about 400 years. To honour his final hours, Sam's year was presenting a special open-air play called *A Site for Sore Eyes*—a history of the school and its grounds through the ages. Fido Tennant was writer and director, and he'd given Sara the leading role of the Chorus—a sort of narrator. Sam was way down on the cast list playing 'Gloomy Monk', some poor bloke from a thousand years ago. His only line was 'Oooh, what a calamity!' when his monastery was washed away in a flash flood.

Sam hadn't yet told Sara about his impending move away. He didn't want to distract her before her starring performance. Not that he was sure she *would* be distracted. Possibly she'd be quite relieved. But he didn't want the news getting out, in case people made a fuss.

Or rather, if he was honest, in case they *didn't* make a fuss.

He sighed.

Sara looked at him, concern showing on her face. 'Look, is something up, Sam?'

'I . . .' Sam shrugged and smiled. 'I just can't believe I have to parade on stage this afternoon dressed as a monk in a *red* habit.'

'Could be *habit*-forming!' Sara forced one of her peculiar horsy laughs. 'See you later, Brother Sam.'

'Probably what the poor old monk's friar said before the flood,' he said gloomily. 'And he was wrong.'

Thinking about it, what the play demonstrated quite worryingly was that every building put up on this land through the ages had ended in disaster. If Sam had been Freekham's headmaster (he shuddered at the mere thought), he would definitely make sure the school's insurance was paid up. Then again, ending up with a school on the site was probably enough of a disaster in itself for the freaky Freekham tradition to hold true. He should be able to get through this last day without the whole school blowing up around him or something. And hopefully without a pigeon dropping its lunch on his shoulder.

Deep in thought, Sam headed off into the playground to track down his friends before the bell for registration, one last time.

As soon as Sara turned from Sam, her smile slipped. She wondered what was on Sam's mind. His brown eyes looked sad, and even his dark spiky fringe was drooping a little. Sam was a total show-off, but maybe he really *was* worried about doing his line in the play. Whatever, she'd decided not to tell him her news just yet. She'd keep it to herself. She'd hate him to be distracted.

Of course, she'd hate him *not* to be distracted even more.

Sara bit her lip. It looked ninety-nine per cent certain now that her mum had got the new job she'd been after, so the Knots would soon be packing up and moving away. Yet another new start, at yet another new school. Sara got through educational establishments like chic clique queen Vicki Starling got through hairspray.

Fido was already in the classroom when she arrived, surrounded by notes and bits of paper. His brown hair was even less tidy than usual, and his blue eyes held a slightly manic stare. He spun round at the sound of the door, a fat black marker pen clutched in one hand like an offensive weapon. 'Sara! There you are!'

'Catch me while you can,' she murmured. She would miss Fido. He was cute, in a slightly random sort of way. 'Everything OK? You look kind of stressed.'

'Just a few last-minute script changes.' He held up a sheet of paper that was soggy with black ink.

'But I just finished learning that!' she protested, walking over and snatching the paper from his hand. Maybe she wouldn't miss him—not with a slap round the chops, at any rate. 'You've changed just about everything!'

'I'm the director,' Fido reminded her snootily. 'Being temperamental, erratic, and brilliant comes with the job!'

'So, when do we get to the brilliant bit?' She half-smiled. 'How did rehearsals go for the last act after school, anyway?'

'Disaster,' muttered Fido. 'Hardly anyone showed—too scared to hang around after school in case the Freekham ghost showed up.' He looked pointedly at her. 'Shame it didn't. I could have got it to read the Chorus.'

'I've come to every other rehearsal,' Sara said defensively. 'My mum wanted me to . . . er . . . help her with something.' *Yeah, help her celebrate getting the new job. 'It's practically in the bag, sweetheart!'—big whoop.* 'But what *is* all this about a Freekham ghost? I've heard a few people talking about it.'

'It's all a load of rubbish,' said Fido. 'Started a few days ago. People reckon they've heard it wailing and clanking about the place. Ashley Lamb thinks it's a spirit teacher we've summoned up by recreating scenes from the school's history.'

'The Ghost of Freekham Past, huh?' Sara raised

an eyebrow. 'Well, there's one sure-fire way of finding out if it truly exists.'

'Oh?'

'Leave Sam alone in a room with it.' She grinned. 'If it hasn't given him a detention in five minutes, it doesn't exist.'

Fido smiled back. 'Come on, let me talk you through the changes I've made to the intro. It's Drama next, you can learn the new lines in time for the dress rehearsal at lunchtime.'

'No pressure, then,' she sighed, scanning the new introduction. 'Come with us on a journey back through the centuries . . . When Freekham was known as Frekkingham, a tiny village noted for its unusually high volume of lunatics, villains, paupers, and rogues. Or in today's language— teachers.' She looked at him. 'We're putting on this play to celebrate Killer Collier's last day victimizing innocent civilians. Do you really think this strikes the right respectful note?'

Fido shrugged. 'It's not like he *wants* to go, is it? He's been pushed! Everyone knows he's past it, himself included—but apparently he begged and begged the Head to let him stay.'

Sara nodded gloomily. Like she'd begged her

mum to let her stay last night. Freekham High was weird all right, but she'd never made so many friends so quickly anywhere else before. That was a good kind of freaky—Memphis, Sam, Fido . . .

'Is this a private funeral or can anyone join in?'

Sara turned and smiled sadly. Talk of the devil—or, more accurately, the beanpole with the shaved head and the coolest sparkle in her wide, green eyes. Memphis Ball was a true one-off. Her uniform was askew, her lips were lipsticky crimson, and everything about her screamed attitude. But if she took to you, Memphis was a bright and dependable friend. Sara looked at her and suddenly her eyes welled up.

Memphis put an arm round her. 'Hey, what's the matter?'

'Yeah, come on, Sara,' said Fido, worriedly. 'I haven't made *that* many changes! You're my leading lady, you can cope!'

'And I'm the prompter,' Memphis reminded her. 'I'll be there for you.'

Sara nodded awkwardly. 'I know, it's not that. It's—'

But just then the bell went for registration. Sara took the script and scooted off to her seat, wiping her eyes frantically on her shirtsleeve so no one else would see her tears. If she really *was* leaving Freekham, no way was she going out as the girly drip who blubbed on her last day.

'I'll tell you later,' she mouthed to Memphis as people started to drift in.

Then, suddenly, the students scattered as Penter marched into the room clutching a battered briefcase. He was an imposing man. His eyes were red-rimmed as if he hadn't slept for a week—and his nasty beard was patchy like he'd finally nodded off while trying to shave it. His hair, on the other hand, was always perfectly combed, as if he'd spent hours over it. It was like seeing a rottweiler with a wig—just . . . *wrong*.

'Come on, everyone, hurry up and sit down!' he snapped, bad-tempered as ever as the last of the crowd straggled inside. 'It may be the end of term but until that final bell goes, you are still school property! Where's Sam Innocent?'

'Maybe he's *lost* property, sir,' quipped Fido, to some laughter.

'His brain's been lost property for years,' added Ruth 'Ruthless' Cook, the class bruiser. She and Sam rarely saw eye to eye—usually because Ruth was trying to punch him in it.

But just as Penter's face began to darken, Sam strolled in. 'Here I am, sir,' he said. 'Just taking a last look round the place . . .' He glanced over at Sara. 'For the summer, I mean.'

'It will *not* be a last look for you, Innocent,' growled Penter. 'Put just one foot out of line and I will give you an after-school detention!'

Sam smiled unexpectedly. 'Do you mean that, sir? Might be kind of nice . . . one more detention, for old times' sake!'

Sara shook her head wearily at Sam's suicidal sense of humour. Penter's red eyes looked as if they were about to shoot lasers at him.

But then, suddenly, a ruffling, cooing wave of noise filled the air and the classroom darkened.

'It's another pigeon attack!' yelled Fido, and the class erupted in chaos.

Some pointed, some screamed, some went very, very pale. Sara settled for cringing.

A whole army of pigeons was flocking at the windows, flapping and jostling as if they wanted to get inside. Each left a little present from its bottom that streaked the glass, blotting out just about everything.

'Help!' wailed Vicki Starling, standing on her chair. 'They want to peck us to pieces!'

'Could they start with Ruth?' Sam grinned.

Ruth was actually hiding behind Ashley Lamb, who seemed to be in a state of shock, staring at the window and sucking furiously on his thumb—a habit Sara thought he had managed to break. She only hoped the pigeons didn't manage to break the windows . . .

'Clear off, you flying vermin!' snarled Penter, marching up fearlessly to the windows. 'Stop making all that mess!' He banged on the glass. 'I'm sick of scrubbing these windows!'

Sam came over to join Sara and Memphis. 'Looks like Penter's in a bigger flap than *they* are,' he chuckled.

'It's so freaky!' Sara complained, staring at the feathered mass of lilac and grey. 'Why are they doing it?'

'Oh, like you don't know,' said Memphis. 'It's the last day of school, and you two will soon be going your separate ways. The gods

13

of freaky had to mark the occasion somehow, didn't—?'

'Separate ways?' Sam interrupted sharply.

'How did *you* know?' Sara said, thinking she'd been rumbled.

She looked at him, and he looked back at her, the pigeons forgotten for a moment.

'Duh. It's the summer holidays,' said Memphis, frowning at the pair of them. 'Unless you were planning on living here by yourselves for the next few months, it's a fair guess that you'll be going your separate ways. And just as well, since you two are the weird-magnets around this place. Maybe the summer will give it a chance to recover.'

Sara laughed weakly and swiftly turned back to the feathered furies at the windows. She hoped Sam hadn't rumbled her. And yet she got the distinct feeling from Sam's shifty behaviour that *he* had something to hide too.

'Go away!' boomed Penter, slapping the register against the glass in a useless attempt to cow the pigeons.

'They want to bruise us all with their wings!' cried Vicki.

'And tangle their feet in our hair!' added Elise, her best friend.

'And steal our ear-rings!' said Denise, her other best friend, not to be outdone.

'And . . .' Therese, last and probably least of Vicki's so-called chic clique, struggled to figure out another foul fowl fate, 'and they want to peck up scraps from the floor next to our feet!' she concluded lamely.

'Save me,' said Sam drily, 'from *that* lot!'

Then, as suddenly as they'd appeared, the pigeons vanished. But they had left a messy legacy of white and black smears, crusting up the windows so completely you couldn't see a thing through them.

'Right!' shouted Penter, surveying his baffled, nervous class. 'Calm down, sit down, and pipe down.'

Fido helped Vicki down from her chair, where she swooned theatrically into the arms of her acolytes. Ruth straightened up quickly. Ashley noticed her and frowned, so she shoved him into his chair and knocked his thumb out of his mouth. 'Don't start *that* again, loser!'

'Back to your desks, quickly now.' Penter

flapped the register at Sara, Sam, and Memphis like a farmer shooing chickens into a run. 'The show is over.'

'Are you sure, sir?' Sam wondered, sitting down beside Ashley. 'With all that bird muck on the glass, they could be performing a song-and-dance number outside and we wouldn't know about it!'

'Well, you, Mr Innocent, will most *certainly* know about it.' Penter smiled, revealing his big yellowy teeth. 'You too, Mr Lamb. You two can clean up the mess!'

'That's not fair!' moaned Sam.

'And while you're doing that to my satisfaction, *I* shall install my patented pigeon-putter-offer.' He opened his briefcase and pulled out a complicated creation of mirrors and string. 'I finished it last night. The sunlight will flash off these pieces of polished glass, confuse the birds, and drive them away from the windows.'

'But it's the last day of term, sir,' said Ashley meekly.

'So why bother?' Sam added.

'Can you imagine what that window will be like after seven more weeks of pigeon attacks?' Penter roared.

'Not sure I want to, sir,' said Sam.

'*You* won't have to imagine,' Penter informed him. 'Because the first thing I'll make you do in the new term is clean it up!'

Sam opened his mouth as if to say something. Then he simply shrugged and smiled sadly. 'Well, whatever you think, sir.'

And right there and then, Sara knew that she wasn't the only one keeping secrets.

PERIODS ONE AND TWO
DOUBLE DRAMA

The bell went for the start of lessons, and Penter took the roll call. Sam watched gloomily as his fellow students bustled off to doss through Drama, while he and Ashley were left alone with their evil teacher.

Penter looked down his nose at them and pressed a key into Ashley's hand. 'Go and fetch a bucket and sponge each from the storeroom.'

'But, sir,' said Ashley nervously, 'the storerooms are *haunted*!'

Penter looked at him in a threatening fashion. 'I beg your pardon?'

'Haunted, sir,' Ashley went on. 'You know, by the Freekham ghost! Couldn't we—'

'Move yourselves!' Penter yelled. 'I'm sick and tired of this nonsense filling the school about ghosts! *Pigeons* are the only things haunting this place—so just fill your buckets with hot water and get wiping away that mess on the windows!'

Ashley gulped and zoomed off at the double. Sam had to jog to keep up with him.

'Slow down,' he complained.

'If we just rush straight in and straight out, maybe the ghost won't notice us,' puffed Ashley.

'Have you actually seen this ghost?' asked Sam. 'Or just heard people going on about it?'

Ashley skittered to a stop, wide-eyed and fearful. 'Bit of both. I've *heard* the ghost!' His thumb started moving to his mouth, until Sam intercepted and pushed it firmly away.

'You've given up. Now, *where* did you hear this ghost?'

'In the storeroom in the Humanities Block, for a start,' said Ashley. 'A low, muffled voice . . . banging on the wall . . . ghostly rumblings . . . Loads of people have heard it in there.'

'Or convinced themselves that they have,' said Sam. 'Some joker was probably hiding inside, killing himself with laughter at your expense. Where else did you hear it?'

'A whole load of us in the debating society

19

heard it at the same time on Wednesday after school,' said Ashley. 'In the old debating rooms. See, I reckon it's the ghost of an old teacher from, like, a century ago maybe—so it only haunts the old parts of the school. The bits that the modern parts have been built around.'

'Well, I suppose that would make sense,' Sam agreed. 'What were you arguing in your debating society, by the way?'

Ashley sighed. 'This house believes that ghosts are figments of the imagination. The motion wasn't carried.'

'Maybe you all just got carried away.' Sam gave him a friendly pat on the shoulder and took the key from his sweaty grip. 'Look, I'll go and get the buckets, OK?'

'OK,' said Ashley quickly.

Sam advanced on the storeroom door. He could hear no sound from within. The key turned, and the door creaked open. Ashley gasped, and Sam gave him a weary look.

Inside it was just an ordinary storeroom like pretty much any other, long and narrow and cluttered with stationery and textbooks—and Penter's promised buckets, worst luck. Not many places for someone to hide. Sam picked up the buckets and locked the door behind him.

'Well, that was truly terrifying,' said Sam, pretending to wipe his brow.

'Other people *have* heard it!' said Ashley firmly. '*Especially* in the Humanities Block.'

'Well, then, I shouldn't worry. Chances are it's turned up to say goodbye to old Collier. If it's a hundred years old, it probably knew him well!' Sam shoved the buckets into his arms with a sigh. 'Now let's go and clean up that poo—before we wind up *in* the poo for taking so long about it!'

Sara felt Memphis's elbow in her ribs as they followed the class to the Drama Studio. 'Care to share what's got you so worked up?'

'Wait till we get inside,' she sighed.

The Drama Studio would be a good place to confess, Sara decided. Its black walls, hanging drapes, and natural wooden floor gave the place a serene and soothing feel.

Usually.

She soon discovered that Fido had raced on

21

ahead of everyone else and was already organizing people the moment they walked in through the door. 'Sara—copy out that script I gave you, and get learning,' he ordered. 'Memphis—can you sort through the costumes in the prop store? The ones with pins in still need some adjustments. Ah, Durbrain, just the bloke I need . . . can you help Thomas and Smithy's group with painting the scenery?'

'S'pose,' said Durbrain, a lanky lad whose long, curly, blond hair, big head and heavy brow gave him the look of a Neanderthal poodle. His real name was Dennis Durban, but his nasty nickname had stuck since he wasn't exactly the sharpest knife in the box. In fact, there were probably baby spoons sharper than he was.

Sara frowned at Memphis. 'Durbrain's not noted for his artistic touch, is he?'

'More like the *Midas* touch,' said Memphis, heading for the costume store. 'You know, turning whatever he touches into gold. If he can do for the backdrops what he did for his Geography coursework, it'll be West End standard.'

'As opposed to *dead*-end standard,' Sara

agreed, looking at the clumsily painted cardboard scenery they'd soon be acting against.

But Memphis was right—it was weird about Durbrain. Collier had graded his coursework for the term and given him an F. It looked for a time as if he was going to have to go to summer school to catch up with the rest of the class. But when he insisted on a re-mark, Collier agreed to look at it again—and this time gave him an A minus!

According to Memphis (school specialist in gossip), the Head had let the new grade stand out of loyalty to Collier, not wanting to embarrass him so close to retirement. But it was obvious that the former 'Killer' was going soft in his very-old-age, and everyone seemed to agree that the sooner he was put out to pasture, the better.

Everyone except Durbrain, of course, who was now sticking up for the old duffer whenever he could.

Just then, Mrs Flange the drama teacher came inside. She had the look of someone who fell through hedges backwards for a living, with her short scruffy hair standing up in every direction and her face fixed forever in a look of mild dismay. 'Everything under control, Fido?' she enquired, clearly hoping for good news.

Fido looked across to where Vicki Starling and her clone drones were working in shifts, slowly, painstakingly cutting out a single cardboard flower. Vicki noticed him tapping his watch. 'What, you think we should risk our manicures?'

'*Sort of* under control, miss,' Fido sighed. 'Though the flowers for the opening meadow scene might be in short supply.'

'I've done ten already,' grunted Ruthless Cook. 'You know, I've always said that flowers are for wimps . . .' She slung a bundle of pink-scribbled cardboard splodges in his direction, and smirked as he picked them up. 'And these are for you— so now I've *proved* it!'

'That's lovely, Ruth, thanks,' sighed Fido. He noticed Sara smiling and scowled at her. 'Learned that script already, have you?'

'No, boss,' Sara admitted. 'Sorry, boss.' She was about to make her way over to a quiet corner when Memphis emerged from behind a backcloth, scratching her shaved head.

'I can't find the blokes' costumes,' she called over to Fido.

'Have you tried using your eyes?' he asked.

Memphis frowned. 'I'll use yours for target practice if you mess. The costumes aren't in the prop store, so where are they?'

Mrs Flange's face fell. 'Are the girls' costumes still there?'

'Yep, we're sorted for skirts, smocks, veils, nurse uniforms, and Ruth's ape costume,' Memphis reported. 'But no sign of any of the boys' gear.'

'You're crazy!' cried Fido, flouncing over to see. He emerged a few seconds later looking pale. 'You're not crazy.'

'Tell me something I don't know,' grumbled Memphis. She glanced over at Sara meaningfully. 'No, that's *your* job.'

'But what are we going to do?' Fido started gnawing his fingernails like a man half-starved. 'We need to get those costume changes made fast. The jester's outfit needs extra pom-poms, and that lunatic outfit is way too big for Smithy. His trousers fell down last time he put them on.'

Sara shuddered. 'Scary thought.'

Mrs Flange shook her head and frowned at Fido. 'Why have you left making these changes so late in the day, Dorian?'

Fido visibly cringed at being called by his real name; he even made his mum call him Fido. 'I've been set back by most of my cast being too scared to make after-school meetings and rehearsals because of the so-called Freekham ghost!' he said, abandoning the nail-biting for a spot of pulling his hair out. 'And now the costumes have gone missing, it's all over. We're doomed!' His voice was rising higher and higher. 'This play's ruined! We're going to be a disaster! We might as well cancel it now!'

'Somebody slap him,' Memphis suggested. 'He's gone hysterical.'

'I'll do it,' Ruth said helpfully.

'He's all right,' said Sara, laying a sympathetic hand on his arm. 'Just having one of his harassed director moments.'

Ruth was undeterred. 'I could slap him anyway.'

'No one is slapping anyone, thank you, Ruth.' Flange chewed her lip for a few moments. 'Got it! Maybe Daisy took them.'

Fido clapped his hands. 'Brilliant! She might

have done, mightn't she? After all, she *is* Chief Costume Designer.'

In fact, Daisy Pellock was the *only* costume designer, Sara reflected, but being a chief looked flashier in the credits on the souvenir programme. Perhaps if they'd had a *real* chief, they could have stopped Daisy making all the costumes red. Sara had to wear a red cape as the chorus, the soldier costumes were all styled on Canadian Mounties, Sam's monk had a red habit . . . even Ruth's ape suit was that of a crimson orang-utan. When challenged, Daisy had claimed she was designing on a theme. In Sara's book, that theme was '*I've only got one idea and a lot of red cloth to use up.*'

'Can we find out what lesson she's in and ask her?' Sara asked.

Flange didn't look keen. 'She'll be here at breaktime anyway, checking everyone's happy with their adjusted costumes.'

'But I can't make any of the adjustments to the boys' costumes till we've got them,' Memphis pointed out patiently.

'Good point,' said Flange. 'Aha! *Here's* someone we can spare to find our girl!'

Sam had come in through the Drama Studio

door. His uniform was splashed with water and nasty white stains, he was red in the face and he didn't look happy.

'I don't know what pigeons eat, but it should be banned under the Human Rights Act,' he said darkly. 'That stuff was like superglue mixed with treacle.'

'Thanks for sharing,' said Fido. 'Now get on your bike and find Daisy Pellock.'

'Is she lost?' Sam wondered.

'Your monk's costume is—along with the rest of the boys' outfits!'

'I'm glad the PE department aren't sponsoring this play,' said Sam, 'or we'd have to act in our vest and pants!'

'So long as they were red,' Sara muttered.

'Daisy Pellock's in the year above, isn't she?' asked Ashley, appearing over Sam's shoulder. 'You should ask at the school office, see if they've got a timetable for her.'

Sam raised an eyebrow. 'Tell you what, Ashley— since you've got all the answers, why don't *you* go?'

'With a ghost roaming the school?' Ashley shuddered. 'You must be bonkers!'

'There's no such thing as ghosts!' shouted Fido.

'He's right,' added Durbrain with surprising passion. 'No such thing.'

'There is too and I've heard one!' Ashley yelled back. 'I bet it's the ghost who took the costumes!'

Sam snorted. 'You reckon it fancied a change from the old sheet and clanking chains look?'

'That's enough!' cried Mrs Flange. 'Now, I want everyone ready for a full run-through in five minutes, with no interruptions—least of all from the world of spirit. Sam, I'll write you a note to explain what you're doing out of lesson should anyone ask—and then you can go and track down Daisy. Find us those costumes!'

'From window cleaner to private eye,' Sam remarked, winking at Sara before departing from the studio. 'Things are looking up!'

'Then watch out for any pigeons overhead!' she called back to him.

It took Sam ages to track down his target. The receptionist in the school office couldn't tell him which form Daisy was in off-hand, so she had to flick through endless files and forms and pieces of paper and even make a couple of phone calls—before finally announcing that Daisy was having English with Miss Bedfellow.

'Which classroom?' Sam asked.

'Oh.' She frowned and looked down at her scattered array of paperwork. 'I don't know. Hold on a minute . . .'

'No, honestly, it's fine,' said Sam quickly, keen to avoid another long search. 'She'll be in the Humanities Block somewhere, won't she?'

'Well, I know they've had to close a couple of the classrooms there, this morning.' She sniffed. 'Nasty chemical smell in there.'

Sam frowned. 'Funny. Humanities is a fair old way from the Science Block. Wonder where the stink came from?'

'Don't ask me,' said the receptionist—as if Sam hadn't learned that lesson already. 'Maybe the ghost made it?'

'You don't believe in it too, do you?' cried Sam.

She shrugged. 'Well, they reckon Humanities is where it's been heard the most, don't they? Ah, here we are. Those classes were moved to the Science Block somewhere.'

'Well, that makes perfect Freekham sense.' Sam nodded. 'Move English into the Science Block because the English classroom *smells* like the Science Block.' He sighed. 'Suppose I'd better track her down.'

As he walked through the twisting, turning corridors that linked many of the blocks together, Sam suddenly heard something: a low, eerie wail of a sound, carrying distantly from somewhere close by. He stopped, straining to listen, but there was nothing.

'Imagination,' he told himself. Besides, there weren't any storerooms round here, and the Science Block was a new part of the school.

Even so, Sam had always noticed a faint smell of must and dust and great age about Freekham High, despite the gleaming floor tiles and bright white ceilings. Sam supposed that the ghost of an old teacher might not approve of these new-fangled buildings. Perhaps that was why it was walking abroad through the school, whinging and complaining like teachers always did, getting in before everyone left for the summer . . .

'*Imagination*,' he insisted out loud, and set off again in search of Daisy.

After several minutes of peering through windows, lurking in corridors, and other generally suspicious behaviour, Sam found Miss Bedfellow's class at last. Bedfellow was one of the better teachers, confident but kind. Sam liked her sharp sense of humour and frizzy dark hair.

'Hi, miss,' Sam said, throwing open the door with a cheery wave. 'I'm here on official business of a very serious nature.'

Miss Bedfellow raised her well-plucked eyebrows. 'Well, Sam, I suggest you get out, knock on the door, wait to be asked inside, be *very* certain you're not wasting my time and that you have official proof of your official business—or you'll be officially on an *extremely* serious detention.' She smiled. 'OK?'

Sam grinned—he also liked her knack for the devastating comeback. Duly retreating, he made a more polite entrance and showed her the note from Flange.

'Well, Daisy,' said Miss Bedfellow. 'Do you know where the boys' costumes might have gone?'

Daisy blinked in surprise. She was a cute

brunette with wide eyes and long straight hair in a ponytail. 'Aren't they in the Drama Studio?'

'Not any more,' said Sam.

'No idea, then,' she said. But then a thought seemed to hit her. 'Oh, hang on, I know another place they might be . . . another *couple* of places actually. Not easy to find though. Miss, is it OK if I go and show him?'

Bedfellow checked her watch and sighed. 'Well, I suppose if it's for the good of the play . . .'

'Cheers, miss,' said Daisy, ignoring the envious looks of her classmates as she got to walk free. 'Catch you later.'

Once they were out in the corridor, Sam turned to her. 'Well? Where are they then?'

Daisy shrugged. 'God knows! I only said I might know to get out of her lesson.'

Sam smiled, quite impressed. 'Quick thinking.'

'I hate these end of term classes,' she said. 'Teachers can't be bothered to start anything new but they won't just let you loose. It's a total waste of time.' Then she started walking off down the corridor. 'See you, then.'

'Oi!' Sam ran after her to catch her up. 'We've still got to find the costumes.'

'They'll turn up,' she said, but he noticed she couldn't seem to look him in the eye. 'I'm meant to be checking them out at break, someone's bound to have found them by then, aren't they?'

'*Are* they?' Sam followed her out into the bright sunlight outside the Science Block. 'Look, Fido's my mate, and he's tearing so much hair out he'll be bald by break if we don't bring him his precious costumes back fast. Are you sure you don't know where they might be?'

Now she looked at him, and her eyes were blazing. 'No, I *definitely* don't know, OK? What are you saying, that I nicked them myself?'

'Course not,' said Sam. 'But can you think of some place they might have ended up by accident? Another storeroom or something?'

Suddenly there was a loud bang from somewhere close by.

'What was that?' Sam turned and tried to trace the sound. It had come from the direction of his very own form room. There were the windows he and Ashley had washed so grumpily

34

earlier this morning. There was the sparkling pigeon-scarer that Penter had hung from the vile, bright green sloping roof of the Science Block, its mirrors flashing in the sunlight as they spun in the breeze.

And there was the fat grey and white body of a pigeon, legs sticking up as it lay on the ground beneath one of those shiny bright windows.

'Oh no!' breathed Daisy. She sprinted over to the crash site and crouched beside the little body. 'It's still alive!'

'Careful!' Sam warned her as he approached. 'Don't touch it!'

'Why? Do you think I might hurt it?'

'No, but you might get fleas or something.' Sam squatted down beside her to see for himself. Clearly the pigeon had got confused by Penter's anti-pidge device and hit the window beak-first. It was stunned, but breathing. 'There's something on its leg,' he noticed. It was a small metal ring. 'Do you think that's like a name tag?'

Daisy took a closer look. 'Nah. It's just letters and numbers—what kind of ID is that?'

'Well, it can't carry a wallet, can it?' Sam

frowned and straightened up. 'This pigeon must belong to somebody. I wonder who?'

'What should we do with it?' asked Daisy. 'Hit it with a brick, put it out of its misery?'

'Stay calm!' he cried, and the pigeon kicked one leg feebly as if in agreement. 'It's just had a shock. A bit of rest, a bit of food and it'll be fine again.' Then he caught sight of the view reflected in the classroom window, and smiled. 'And there's the perfect pet pigeon hotel.'

Daisy looked at him blankly. 'Where?'

'The school farm!' Sam gestured to the buildings and barns with the high fence at the end of a long, concrete path. He should have thought of it sooner—there was an excellent view of the school farm from his form room; he stared out at it each morning. 'Mr Ferret keeps a few pigeons there, doesn't he? I bet this is one of his.' He gently scooped it up with both hands. It didn't struggle. 'Even if it's not, he'll know what to do with it.'

'Ferret's not there,' Daisy said quickly.

'Isn't he?'

'No, he's been off sick, I think. I don't know if anyone will be there, now.'

'You have such a bright and sunny outlook on life, don't you,' sighed Sam.

She shrugged. 'Anyway, I thought you were worried about fleas?'

'Only for your sake. *I've* already got them.' He smiled, but she just looked blankly at him. 'Anyway, that was before I saw the poor little thing. He's kind of sweet, don't you reckon?' The pigeon looked up at him with black beady eyes, its feathers soft and downy against his fingers and he cooed at it. 'I'll check the farm out, just in case there's anyone there who can help. Otherwise I'll get the school office to phone a vet or something.'

The loud, blaring hooter sounded for the start of break. 'I should get off to the Drama Studio,' Daisy announced. 'See if the costumes have turned up.' She raised a hand and hurried away. 'Later.'

'Yeah, later,' said Sam, watching her go and puzzled by her sudden urgency. Then he set off for the farm, carrying the pigeon as carefully as he could, with a little spring in his step.

It looked as if his last day at Freekham High was shaping up to be another weird one—a little send-off from the freakiest school he'd ever known. Cool. He was glad he was going out with a bang, and not with a whimper.

But then, he really had no idea what was in store . . .

BREAKTIME

'And then, at precisely 19.41 on the 19th of April 1941, a German Messerschmitt dropped several bombs on the old Freekham Grammar School—causing . . .' Sara racked her brains, trying to remember her line, 'causing . . .'

Memphis was kneeling on the Drama Studio floor beside her. 'Want a prompt?'

'Hang on,' said Sara, concentrating hard. '. . . a German Messerschmitt dropped several bombs on the old Freekham Grammar School—causing thousands of pounds worth of *improvements* to the general area!'

'That's right!' Memphis grinned. 'Fido's script is going to raise a few eyebrows, isn't it?'

Sara nodded. 'I wonder if Collier's going to be laughing? He was already teaching at Freekham when the Germans came calling. It was that bomb dropping that persuaded him to join the army.'

Memphis smiled. 'Surprised they let him in. I bet he was all old and wrinkly even then!'

'Apparently he stayed fighting for the rest of the war.'

'And hasn't stopped since.'

Then the klaxon sounded for the end of the lesson. 'No sign of our chief costume designer,' Sara observed. 'So much for Sam Innocent, Private Eye.'

'Public Menace, more like.' Memphis grinned. 'I shudder to think what he's been up to.' Her smile faded. 'But what about you? What's going on there—the tears this morning, the long face . . .'

Sara sighed. 'Looks like my mum's found another job,' she whispered. 'Somewhere a long way from here. This could be my last day.'

'Oh my God!' Memphis yelled, causing everyone to look over. Vicki and her chic clique were closest. 'I . . . uh . . . broke a nail,' she told them. At once their faces crinkled with kind understanding, and they returned to their delicate flower production line.

'Girls,' said Flange, despairingly, 'we could *grow* the flowers more quickly . . .'

Memphis turned back to Sara and lowered her voice so that Smithy, Thomas, Durbrain, and Ruth—who were painting some scenery nearby—couldn't hear them. 'You're leaving Freekham? So soon?'

'Mum's pretty positive we'll be off within a month or so. It didn't really work out for her here.' Sara shrugged. 'Unlike me. Despite all the weird stuff, I've never been as happy anywhere else.'

'Oh, this stinks! I'll really miss you, Sara . . .'

'And me you.'

Memphis smiled sadly. 'Hey, what about Sam?'

'What about him? He'll still be around, causing chaos.'

'I mean, have you told him?'

'Not yet,' said Sara firmly. 'I don't want him to know.'

'Why not?' asked Memphis.

'I just *don't*. Not till after the play, 'K? I don't even want to *think* about any of this till then.'

'I know why you don't want to tell him you're leaving.' Memphis gave Sara a penetrating stare, as if she was peering right inside. 'You're worried he won't be as upset about it as you are.'

'You're crazy,' Sara protested, as she felt herself go red. Luckily, just at that point the door opened—and in came Daisy with a face like thunder.

'Daisy!' cried Fido, welcoming her like some long-lost relative. 'So Sam found you! What about the costumes?'

'Sam found a pigeon,' she said loudly, looking around the room. 'A crashed one, lying on the ground outside the Science Block. It was white and grey and its leg was tagged. He's taken it to the farm.'

Memphis frowned. 'Did I miss the bit where we asked her for her life story?'

But Daisy's tale seemed to have a dramatic effect on Durbrain. He suddenly got up from his backdrop and stormed out of the studio.

'What's up with him?' wondered Sara.

'More to the point, what's up with these splodges?' Memphis was looking at the scenery he'd left behind. It was a painting of a big stone wall, the one constant backdrop for their open-air stage, in front of which all other scenery would be arranged. But all along the top of the wall, Durbrain had daubed large, bright-red circles.

42

'They're poppies,' grunted Ruth. 'Or sun-flowers, or something.'

'They look a right mess,' said Memphis.

Flange cleared her throat. 'Actually, they symbolize the vibrant and resilient nature of this patch of ground our school stands upon.'

Sara stared. '*Durbrain* said that?'

'Well, no,' Fido admitted. 'He just decided to paint a bunch of red splodges—and we had to explain them away somehow, didn't we? Anyway, they're the least of our worries.' He looked desperately at Daisy. 'We've *got* to find those costumes!'

'I'm sure they'll turn up,' said Daisy. Sara was surprised the girl wasn't more anxious, considering all the work she'd put into creating those costumes. Instead, she just seemed kind of sullen.

'I've been through the female costumes and fixed what I could, but I'm not the greatest with needle and thread,' Memphis told Daisy. 'They're in the prop store. Want to check you're happy with them . . . chief?'

If Daisy noticed the gentle tease in Memphis's voice she didn't react. 'Thanks, I will,' she said, and walked off to see.

'Maybe we *should* do the play in our vest and pants,' sighed Fido. 'All of us. No costumes at all.' He perked up slightly. 'Yeah, we could call it, "The History of Freekham—laid bare"!'

Memphis frowned. 'Or we could lock you up right now in a padded room for your own safety.'

'The costumes have to be somewhere. We'll just have to organize a super-search of the whole school,' Flange declared. 'I'll get the keys for all the storerooms from Mr Biggins and we'll leave no stone unturned.'

'I'm up for that,' said Sara. 'My head's so stuffed full of lines right now, I could do with a little distraction.'

'You could do with another read-through,' said Fido. 'Perhaps if I—'

'Give it a rest, Dorian!' said Flange. 'We'll get the costumes and sets all sorted, then have a full dress rehearsal at lunchtime. All right?'

'S'pose so,' said Fido sulkily. 'Where's Sam? He should be helping us out, not pratting about with a poorly pigeon!'

'Yeah, where is he?' wondered Sara. It didn't look as if she was going to see much of him today. Not that it mattered . . . not at all . . .

Obviously.

Sam walked swiftly over to the school farm, awkwardly straddling the low front gate so he didn't have to let go of the dazed pigeon. 'Farm' was possibly too grand a term for it—it was basically a small classroom block, surrounded by several paddocks. There were two cows, one goat, four pigs, and a couple of sheep, as well as a pigeon loft and several bird houses. Should the school ever burn down they would have one hell of a barbecue.

As he approached the main doors to the block, Sam noticed that the blinds in Ferret's office were closed. That was a good sign, he felt—someone must surely be in if they wanted to keep out the sun's glare. Then his foot brushed against something on the floor. It was a photograph; an aerial photograph of the school and the playing fields, taken from somewhere way up high in the air. Where had *that* come from?

Shrugging, Sam pressed on. The main doors

led into a small entrance hall. To Sam's left was the door to Ferret's office, its window blanked with black sugar-paper. Straight ahead was the doorway to one classroom, and to his right was the doorway to another.

It was this door that burst open—to reveal Killer Collier.

'What do you want, boy?' he roared. He was dressed, as ever, in his dusty blue pinstripe suit. He had a face like an old apple that had learned to grow a moustache, and eyebrows like bushy white caterpillars. But despite being short, wrinkled, and ancient, there was something about him that commanded fear and respect. Sam didn't know a single student who wasn't wary of this tough old bird—himself included.

'Well, don't just stand there staring, lad! What is it?'

'I found this outside the Science Block, sir,' Sam stammered, holding out the pigeon. 'It flew into a window.'

Collier frowned, and with surprising speed, scooped up the stricken pidge. 'You're holding him wrong,' he grumbled, sliding one hand under the bird's belly from the front, scissoring his

46

fingers so its legs stuck through, and hooking his thumb over the bird's body from above to stop its wings from moving. Then he held it close to his chest with surprising care.

'Didn't know you were an expert, sir,' said Sam, truly impressed.

'Used to handle these little chaps in World War Two,' he said fondly. 'Used them to send messages between platoons in Madagascar.'

'Er, where's that, sir?'

Collier shot him a look with his watery blue eyes. 'No, of course, no one remembers all that we fought for any more. No one cares. They just sweep us aside when we're too old to be of any use.'

Sam was taken aback by the outburst. He was still groping around for something to say when another man appeared, looming in the classroom doorway. Incredibly, this bloke seemed even older than Collier. From the expression on his gaunt face, he might have just sat on a spike, and, from the way he was holding himself so straight, it might be a very long one.

'That's enough, Collier,' the man boomed. 'We'll have no displays of emotion. Keep a proper military bearing, man!'

'Yes, sir,' Collier barked. 'Er, Quentin, I mean.' He looked a bit shifty as he turned back to Sam. 'This is an old army friend of mine, Mr Pacemaker. He's a supply teacher. I brought him in to hold the fort while Mr Ferret is away.'

'Right,' said Sam uncertainly. Pacemaker looked more like an about-to-die teacher than a supply teacher. 'Nice to meet you, sir.'

'You up to something, boy?' roared Pacemaker, advancing threateningly. 'What brings you here, eh?'

'He's brought in a wounded pigeon,' said Collier, passing the bird to his friend.

'Casualty of war, eh?' Pacemaker handled it in the same easy fashion and inspected it closely through a monocle.

'There's a tag on its leg, sir,' said Sam helpfully. 'MVPA-05-something-something—'

'We don't need a tag to know where it came from, boy,' growled Collier.

'Shock!' Pacemaker almost yelled his diagnosis. 'Bash on the beak. Soon recover!'

With that, he marched off back into the classroom.

'Look here, Innocent,' said Collier, mumbling

48

through his moustache as if he was suddenly embarrassed. 'Could I ask you to keep quiet about this? The pigeon's one of Mr Ferret's. It must have escaped the lofts here by accident and I don't want my old chum Mr Pacemaker getting into trouble on our last day.' He looked at Sam directly. 'Will you promise to keep this a secret?'

Sam blinked in amazement. He'd never seen Collier show a softer side before—with the possible exception of Durbrain's A minus. 'Er . . . OK,' he agreed. 'Why not?'

'Good chap,' said Collier, his moustache twitching now as he smiled. 'Run along, now, eh?'

Sam emerged from the school farm in as much of a daze as the pigeon. Somehow, Collier acting as if he was human and not just a teacher seemed freakier than anything else that had ever happened at Freekham High.

On his way out, he noticed the photo of Freekham from above again. He smiled and picked it up. There was a sort of red stain over part of the playing fields, but that didn't matter. If his dad really *was* moving them away, then he could keep it as a little souvenir. And if by some miracle they *didn't* go, well then—he could always pin it up on his bedroom door and throw darts at it.

Sara and Memphis were walking through the deserted Humanities Block, armed with a set of keys and a note from Flange which was like diplomatic immunity—a licence to be anywhere in the school, no matter what any over-eager prefect or bored teacher might have to say about it.

'Of course, you realize that the humanities storeroom is where the ghost has been heard the most?' said Memphis as they neared their destination.

'I realize that something stinks round here,' said Sara, as a strong pong of chemicals swamped her nostrils.

The storeroom was sandwiched between two classrooms, both of which had signs hanging on the doors—CLOSED UNTIL FURTHER NOTICE.

'Someone must have had an accident,' said Memphis.

Sara nodded. 'But what would chemicals be doing out of the Science Block?'

'P'raps the ghost fetched them?'

'Memph, stop it! There's no such thing as ghosts.'

'Hope not.' Memphis unlocked the storeroom door and nudged it open. The smell was even worse in here.

'Ugh!' Sara held her nose as she groped round for the light switch. 'That is horrible!'

But the light didn't work. The room remained steeped in darkness.

'Typical,' said Memphis.

'Well, it's bright enough out in the corridor. Our eyes will soon adjust.' Sara looked around the storeroom as its dark shapes and outlines began to show detail. A filing cabinet stood in shadow, against the back wall, flanked by a small stack of chairs. Shelves lined the other two walls from floor to ceiling, loaded with school supplies like pens and paper and exercise books. A vacuum cleaner, small and round with a long hose, guarded the entrance.

'Don't see the costumes anywhere,' said Sara, stepping over the contraption and peering more closely at the shadows. 'Unless maybe they're inside the filing—'

She broke off as a low, muffled sigh sounded eerily from the darkness ahead of her.

'Oh. My. God,' hissed Memphis behind her.

Sara made a rapid retreat, and fell backwards over the vacuum cleaner. 'It—it's just the wind,' she stammered as Memphis helped her up. 'Or else . . . er . . .'

The frightening groan sounded again from the storeroom. Sara and Memphis grabbed hold of each other and yelled in alarm. Then Memphis booted the door shut, Sara spun the key in the lock, and they turned and fled. Only once they were back outside in the sunlight, in the middle of the playground, surrounded by the comforting rush and chatter of people enjoying Break did they stop to catch their breath.

'So,' gasped Memphis. 'That was weird.'

Sara's legs felt like half-eaten jelly. 'That was just a figment of our imagination or something.'

'It was something all right. Pure freakiness!'

'Trust this place not to let me slip off without something mad happening,' Sara groaned. 'But . . . well, I mean . . . There's got to be a perfectly normal explanation.' She looked at Memphis hopefully. 'Hasn't there?'

'I guess,' said Memphis. 'But one thing we *do* know—didn't seem to be any missing costumes in there. So should we look in one of the other storerooms?'

They looked at each other for a few seconds, then spoke in unison: 'Nuh-uh!'

Laughing with nerves, excitement, and relief, they headed back to the Drama Studio. 'Sam will never believe us! He'll think we've gone crazy,' Sara gabbled. 'I can't wait to tell him . . .'

But as they arrived back at the Drama Studio, she realized that if she wanted to speak to Sam, she would have to get in line.

Penter had beaten them to it. And he didn't look happy. He was bearing down on Sam in the middle of the studio; everyone else had left apart from Fido and Flange who were watching in concern.

'The simple facts are these, Innocent,' snarled Penter. 'Valuables have been taken from the headmaster's office this morning, and someone wearing a red medieval monk costume was spotted close by.'

Sara turned to Memphis in surprise. 'That's where one of the missing costumes went!'

'Mrs Flange informs me that you, Innocent, are playing the part of this monk in the play,' boomed Penter, 'and so you are my number one suspect! Do you have anything to say?'

PERIOD THREE
HISTORY

Sam stared up at the belligerent bearded bully and gave his most winning smile. 'It wasn't me, sir,' he said calmly. 'Once I'd finished cleaning the windows for you, I came here—as Mrs Flange will tell you—and then I went to the school office, dressed as myself—as the receptionist will tell you—and then I went off to the Humanities Block looking for Daisy Pellock—as Miss Bedfellow will tell you—and then I—'

Just then the klaxon went for the end of Break. Sam broke off, thinking fast. He had made a promise to Collier that he would say nothing about Ferret's pigeon escaping for the sake of creepy Pacemaker. And although promises to teachers were worthless, there was something so pathetic about the way Collier had acted that made Sam reluctant to betray his confidence . . .

The klaxon stopped. Penter raised a ragged eyebrow. 'Yes?'

Sam shrugged. 'Then I found a pigeon that almost killed itself on your anti-pigeon trap—as the pigeon will tell you, if it ever opens its beak again—and then it was Break and here I am.'

Penter's face began to darken, but luckily Flange came to his rescue. 'All the boys' costumes have gone missing, Mr Penter,' she said.

'So?' Penter was unimpressed. 'He could have taken them first thing this morning.'

'I was with him, sir,' said Sara. 'The whole time.' Sam looked at her and smiled. Good old Sara. He would miss her.

'Who actually saw this thieving monk, sir?' asked Fido.

'The Head's secretary,' said Penter.

'Did she get a good look?' asked Flange.

Penter looked cross. 'No. She thought she'd seen that ridiculous school ghost and hid at once behind a wastepaper basket.'

'She might well have seen it,' Sara piped up. 'We *heard* it!'

Sam frowned. '*You* did?'

'There is no such thing as the Freekham

56

ghost!' yelled Penter. Then he turned back to Sam. 'All right, Innocent, I can't prove that you're not . . . er . . . innocent. But I'll get to the bottom of this. And I'll be keeping a close eye on you.'

'I appreciate your concern, sir,' beamed Sam.

'Get off to your next lesson,' Penter snapped. 'All of you!'

Once Penter had gone, everyone seemed to start breathing again, even Mrs Flange.

Sam looked at Sara and Memphis. 'I only came back here to find you two,' he complained. 'Walked right into that ambush!'

'You OK, mate?' asked Fido.

'I won't be sorry to be saying goodbye to *him*. For the summer, I mean,' he added hastily.

'At least we know the costumes must be around somewhere,' sighed Flange.

'And they'll be too hot to hang on to now the thief's been spotted in the monk outfit,' said Fido. 'So hopefully they'll be dumped somewhere easy to find. How many storerooms did you check, Sara?'

'Er . . . just the one,' she said.

Memphis nodded. 'Humanities Block.'

Sam stared at them doubtfully. 'What's all this about you hearing the ghost?'

'It was moaning, sort of like it was in pain,' said Sara. 'Honest!'

'I never thought I'd agree with anything Penter said,' said Fido, his voice rising to a frustrated yell that echoed round the Drama Studio, 'but there is *no such thing as the Freekham ghost*!'

'All right, Dorian, that's enough,' said Flange, who looked as though she had a major-league headache coming on. 'Take it outside, I've got another class now, and I'll get them on to finishing the last of the scenery.'

'Can I search the school for the costumes?' Fido pleaded, with a glare at Sara and Memphis. 'Since my star and her prompter could only find a ghost!'

Flange shook her head. 'I'm going to ask Mr Biggins to search for them. If a thief has taken the costumes, it's better you don't get involved.'

'Oh, but, miss—'

'Out! Now!' she ordered, shooing them through the door. 'Fido, if you come back at Breather I'll let you know if I've had any luck.

The rest of you, I'll see you here at lunchtime for a dress rehearsal.'

'Or an undress rehearsal, in the boys' case,' sighed Sam.

He, Sara, Memphis, and Fido trudged along the corridors towards History.

'Are you serious about this ghost thing?' Sam demanded suddenly.

'Serious about something,' said Sara cautiously.

'We smelt it as well as heard it,' Memphis told him. 'A weird, chemical smell.'

Sam smirked. 'That's all over the Humanities Block. I can even smell it here!'

'They do say that a weird smell out of nowhere is a sign there's a spirit about,' said Sara.

'*White* spirit, if you ask me,' said Sam. 'This whole thing is just someone playing an end-of-term prank,' he insisted, 'like taking those costumes and robbing the Head.'

'Not a very funny prank,' muttered Fido.

'Why would anyone steal the costumes just so they could steal from the Head's office?' wondered Sara.

'Didn't want to be recognized, did they,' said Sam.

'No, I mean, why take a chance nicking the costumes just to nick something else? Why not bring their own disguise?'

'Perhaps they didn't know they wanted to steal something until this morning,' Memphis suggested.

'But how would they know where the costumes were, anyway?' asked Fido. 'Only us lot knew they were in the costume store . . .'

Memphis looked interested. 'You think it was someone in our class?'

'Stay calm,' said Sam. 'If anyone was looking to dress up in this school, they'd try the Drama Studio first, wouldn't they? Regular classrooms aren't exactly famous for their wardrobes.'

'But why take *all* the costumes?' wondered Sara.

Sam grinned. 'Maybe there's a whole load of thieves wandering about this school right now in full costume and make-up!' He stopped suddenly, as an idea zapped into his brain. 'Or maybe, whoever wanted to go nicking from the Head sent someone else out to find a costume for them . . . and that someone took a whole load of them to be sure they had something which would fit!'

'Makes sense,' said Fido slowly. 'But who?'

'That's what we need to find out,' said Sara.

Memphis smiled a little nervously. 'Unless it *is* the ghost, of course.'

'Leave it!' Fido warned her. 'But speaking of unlikely stories, Sam, what's all this about a pigeon?'

'It clonked its head on our classroom window, thanks to Penter.' He scowled. 'I'd like to see a flock of pigeons pick him up and smack him into a bird table, see how he likes it!'

'Pigeons are horrible things.' Sara shuddered. 'Rats with wings.'

'This one was tagged,' Sam informed her. 'So it was a racing pigeon—or do I mean a homing pigeon?' He shrugged. 'Clever, anyway.'

Sara didn't look convinced. 'If it *was* clever, it would have missed the window.'

'What did you do with it?' asked Fido.

'Thought it might be one of Ferret's, so I took it to the school farm. He wasn't there but . . .' Sam raised his eyebrows as they turned the corridor into the Humanities Block, 'but *he* was.'

There, outside one of the closed classrooms,

was Killer Collier. And he was talking to Durbrain. No, from the looks of it, talking wasn't quite the right word.

It was as if they were in conference.

'Durbrain suddenly tore off from the Drama Studio, didn't he?' said Memphis. 'When Daisy started on about the pigeon. She didn't hang on for long herself after that, come to think of it.'

'Well, it *was* Break time,' Sara reminded her.

'What's he talking to Collier about?' wondered Fido. 'Trying to get his classwork re-graded to an A minus the way his coursework was?'

'That was totally dodgy, wasn't it,' Sam agreed.

'Maybe he's just saying a fond farewell,' said Memphis. 'Let's face it, he's never going to get a grade that good again.'

'Not unless he digs up some dirt on the teacher,' joked Sam. But then he saw the others were looking at him. 'What?'

'Maybe he's dug up something on Killer!' whispered Sara excitedly. 'Maybe he blackmailed the old boy into giving him that better mark!'

Sam looked at the way Collier and Durbrain were talking, quietly and seriously. 'Killer doesn't look like he's being blackmailed,' he observed.

'But they do seem to have a lot to talk about, don't they?'

'Excuse me!' came a voice like thunder from along the corridor. 'Can I expect you all in my lesson any time soon?'

They looked up to find that Horrible Hayes, their History teacher, had emerged from his classroom and was glaring at them all. Hayes was one of those teachers who shouldn't be scary, but somehow was. He was a small, slight man, barely taller than Sam, with short black hair and a neatly groomed moustache and beard. His evil stare, magnified by his square, thick-rimmed glasses, could probably bore holes in you—and his lessons could *definitely* bore the pants off you in under ten minutes.

'Coming, sir,' said Sara, speaking for them all.

Just then Hayes noticed Killer Collier staring at him indignantly. 'Sorry, Mr Collier,' he said respectfully. 'I didn't mean to interrupt you.'

Now Killer looked at Durbrain as though he'd just floated up from a sewer. 'Our discussion is ended,' he said simply, and shuffled off on his way.

Durbrain hurried into the classroom looking

shifty and red-faced, and Sam, who was the last to enter, wondered why. But then the sharp, acrid stink in the classroom hit him and all thoughts evaporated except for one: 'Pwoo-oo-aaarrr! What a whiff!'

'That's enough,' snapped Hayes, although he did open the windows still further.

As Sam took his place next to Thomas Doughty, he saw the rest of the class were finding it hard to cope too. Thomas's shirt was pulled up over his nose. At the next desk, Ginger Mutton and Michelle Harris were slumped in their seats, pulling faces at the pong.

'Shouldn't this classroom be closed, sir, like the other two?' Sam asked.

'A nasty niff never hurt anyone,' Hayes insisted. 'I will not tolerate disruption to my lessons, not even on the last day of term.'

'Where do you dink duh smell is gumming from, dir?' asked Smithy, holding his nose at the back of the class, next to Fido.

'It'll be a whiff of old chemicals caught in the air vents, I expect,' said Hayes airily. 'This part of the school was built around the original science block.'

'The one that was blown up in the war?' asked Ruth Cook eagerly.

'Yes. It was taken over by the army for a while; they stockpiled supplies here,' said Hayes, never one to miss out on a chance to numb you with his favourite subject. 'The bomb that fell did a lot of damage and materials weren't easy to come by, so they patched it up as best they could, and rebuilt it properly after the war.'

'I think I'll put a bit of that into the play, sir,' said Fido.

'Not *more* for me to learn!' groaned Sara, resting her head against her desk.

'In any case, the smell will soon clear, I'm sure,' said Hayes. 'So I'd like to continue our work on the Franco-Prussian war with the siege of Paris in 1870 . . .'

'But, sir!' Ruth protested. 'It's the last day of term!'

'And unless you want to spend it in detention, Cook, shut up and get your books out!' he roared.

Sam sighed and got his own books out. Hayes wasn't famous for his holiday spirit.

'Now, by September 1870, the Prussians had

shut down all telegraph and postal services in and out of Paris,' Hayes went on. 'Those trapped within the besieged city made desperate attempts to keep up communications. Five sheepdogs were floated out by balloon with the intention of carrying back mail. None of them were ever seen again.'

'Duh!' Thomas Doughty grinned at Sam. 'Can you blame them for doing a runner?'

'Their great-great-great-great-great grandpuppies are probably still running their own successful ballooning business,' Sam agreed.

Hayes was still droning on: 'An attempt to put the post into zinc balls and float them down the River Seine also failed.'

'They were *in*-Seine if they thought that would ever work!' Sam chuckled. 'What a load of—'

'Which meant that the only reliable source of getting information in and out of the capital was by carrier pigeon,' Hayes concluded. 'Over one million messages travelled in this way during the four month siege.'

Sam shut up and listened.

'Pigeons have an excellent sense of location and direction,' the teacher explained, 'and can be trained to always return home to their lofts, even over great distances.'

Right on cue, a flock of pigeons swooped past the window. They looked like birds on a mission. Pigeons with a job to do. Sam thought of the photo he had found outside the school farm, and realized that the view of the school from high above showed Freekham High exactly as a pigeon might see it.

PERIOD FOUR
BIOLOGY

After thirty minutes of bum-numbing boredom and chemical whiffs, Sara felt like punching the air when the mad, blaring hooter sounded the end of period three. Maybe another school might not be so bad after all. Her head was aching, the lines she had tried to learn were whirling about in her brain, and her nose was ready to fall off.

'At least it's Biology next,' sighed Memphis as they trooped out of the smelly classroom and fell into step with Fido and Sam. 'That will be a doss.'

Sara nodded. 'And at least it's a long way from this stink! How could some chemicals just spill into the air vent?'

Memphis looked at her meaningfully and was about to open her mouth when Fido nudged her in the ribs. 'Don't say it was the ghost!' he warned her.

'The storeroom's only just down the corridor,' Memphis told him. 'Go and see it—or hear it—for yourself.'

Suddenly, Durbrain came up behind them. 'There's no such thing as the Freekham ghost!' he said, glaring at Memphis from under his heavy brow. 'So drop it, slaphead!'

'Were we talking to you? I don't think so,' said Memphis. 'Anyway, I'd sooner be a slaphead than have hair like a poodle in curlers!'

Durbrain went off scowling, and Sara watched him go. 'He's a weird one, Durbrain, isn't he? Tries his hardest not to do a scrap of work each day, upsets most people he comes across . . . and yet he was really keen to paint that scenery.'

'That's because he was doing it for me and not some teacher.' Fido smiled. 'As the director of this play I inspire everyone around me.'

'Yeah, inspire them to have total mental breakdowns,' said Memphis.

'Oi! Sam's not having a total mental breakdown,' said Fido, thwacking him round the head. 'He's totally mental already. Aren't you?'

'What? Oh yeah. Totally,' Sam agreed, distracted.

Sara looked at him uncertainly. 'You're very quiet.' She placed a caring hand on his arm. 'Everything OK?'

'I was just thinking about pigeons.'

'Oh,' said Sara, snatching her hand away.

'See?' said Fido. '*Completely* mental!'

'Hayes was saying they can be trained,' Sam went on. 'And I was thinking, that lot this morning, arriving together to poo all over the window . . .'

Memphis stared. 'You think they were trained to poo in unison?'

'In *poo*-nison,' Sam corrected her.

'And yet you won't believe in the—'

'Leave it,' said Fido threateningly.

'Why would anyone want to train pigeons to poo all over a window?' asked Sara, baffled.

'You're the one who's full of poo, Sam!' teased Fido. 'Come on, we may as well get Cabbage's lesson out the way. I only hope Flange and Biggins have found the stolen costumes by now.'

They soon reached the Science Block. 'Cabbage' Kale was standing in the doorway to his classroom with a party hat jammed on his black mop of hair and wearing a clown's nose—although in fact it was only a little rounder and redder than the one it disguised. He was one of those teachers who thought they were wacky but who were really just lame-o. The funniest thing about Cabbage was his super-deep cleft chin, which looked more like he was carrying round a miniature bum beneath his lips.

'Welcome to the last Biology lesson of the term,' he cried as the class trudged dutifully inside. 'Thought we'd do some *clowning around* today!' He tapped his nose when no one laughed. 'Get it?'

'Nice one, sir,' sighed Sam.

'It's red, it smells, it's picked in the garden,' he said, swinging his head round the class for any signs of reaction, like a hopeful dog. 'No, not my nose, you muppets—my *rose*!' He pulled a red rose in a vase from behind his back and guffawed. 'I may be a teacher, but I'm crazy with it!'

'That's one word for it,' Sara cringed as she settled into her seat beside Memphis.

Kale meanwhile was still wiping tears of mirth

from his eyes when a strange, sinister clanking noise started up. It was quiet and distant—but as the whole class fell silent, it seemed suddenly louder. CLANG-CLANK-CLANG . . . KA-CLANG . . .

'What's that?' gasped Vicki Starling.

'What's what?' said Durbrain stubbornly.

'That clanking noise,' said Ruth.

'It's the ghost!' wailed Therese.

'There is no such thing as the Freekham ghost!' snapped Durbrain.

Sara turned to Fido, who was usually first in with that observation, but he was holding his head to one side, listening closely. 'It's coming from the walls!'

'It's our imaginations,' suggested Doubting Thomas.

'It's nothing,' said Durbrain, going one further.

'It sounds like it's coming from beneath us,' said Sam, ignoring them both as he slipped from his stool and pressed his ear to the floor. But he was forced to call a sudden halt to his analysis when Ruth seemed about to step on his head.

'Everyone chill out,' said Kale, as a wave of

astonished chatter started to drown out the eerie noise. 'It's just something mechanical. The old boiler, probably.' He paused to slap his own wrist. 'Oooh, I must not talk about my mother-in-law like that!'

The rubbish joke achieved what Kale could not—the class fell silent. They all listened out for the noise again, but it had stopped.

Sara frowned. 'It can't be the boiler, sir. The heating's not on today.'

'Exactly!' said Cabbage triumphantly. 'But it was last night! I heard Mr Biggins say its timer was up the spout. That clanking's probably the sound of the pipes cooling down. That's all.'

'Pipes,' Sam echoed thoughtfully. 'They must run under the ground, connecting all the buildings together, for water and that.'

'Like veins under the skin, feeding the whole body of the school,' Kale agreed. 'I'll make a biologist out of you yet, Sam.'

'I don't think you will, sir,' said Sam, but there was something sad about his smile. Memphis had noticed too. She was watching Sam in that cool, detached way of hers.

'Anyway, let's clear out of this stuffy old

classroom and its funny noises, shall we?' said Cabbage brightly. 'Since it's the last day of term, I thought it might be a laugh to study how the human respiration system works under pressure in high temperatures—' he suddenly produced a rounders bat and ball from under his desk— 'by running about and playing some ball games outside!'

At this announcement, the mood of the class lifted. Sporty Doubting Thomas practically pounced on the bat and ball, and once Cabbage had taken off his party hat and silly nose, he led the way out through the science block and into the sweltering sunshine, a huge, red, furled umbrella stuffed under one arm.

Sara frowned. 'Expecting rain, sir?'

'Just shading my head,' he told her. 'I got sunstroke once. Turned me mental—not that my wife noticed for a fortnight!' He spluttered with mirth and started jogging down the path towards the playing fields. 'Come on, then! I saw some of Mr Wigmore's woodwork students this morning, putting up the stage for this afternoon's show. We can use it as a pitcher's mound and play baseball!'

'Do we have to go all that way, sir?' complained Durbrain. 'Why can't we play down the near end?'

'Clearly, you've never seen me bat, Dennis,' cried Cabbage. 'A home run every time! I'd be breaking every window in the sports hall if we played there . . .'

Out in the sunshine, Sara found it easy to forget about the spooky noises in the classroom. She had more pressing problems. As she traipsed after Kale and her classmates up the slope to the playing fields, her heart began to thud in her chest. She could see the stage dead ahead across the sea of grass—the same stage she would soon be prancing on. And she realized she was dreading it. Everything suddenly seemed such a rush.

Would she remember her lines?

Would the scenery dry in time?

Would the boys have any costumes to wear, or would Sam be playing a monk with no habit at all besides his many bad ones?

She could see Fido was looking just as worried as she was. Sam didn't look very cheerful either— was he OK, or just still deep in thought about pigeons? Maybe she should tell him the news of her leaving Freekham—that would really give him something to think about . . .

Wouldn't it?

Cabbage came to a stop in front of the surprisingly sturdy-looking stage and put up his enormous red golfing umbrella.

'Sir, you don't need to use that thing,' said Durbrain, wriggling uncomfortably as if he had ants in his pants. 'Why don't you just sit at the back of the stage where it's shady?'

Cabbage chortled. 'Your concern for my welfare is touching, Dennis—but no, you *can't* be a team captain!'

'But, sir—'

'You and Thomas can take four chairs and mark out the bases.' He pointed to two stacks of plastic chairs at the back of the stage. 'Sara, you can do the team-picking honours—together with your other half, Sam!'

'He's not my other half!' Sara protested as classmates nearby laughed and wolf-whistled.

'Please, sir!' called Durbrain as he marked fourth base with the last chair, his fat features wedged into an expression of sheer dismay. 'Can

I use your umbrella to mark out the diamond in the grass?'

'Don't think the Head will be happy when he comes out here this afternoon and finds you've been carving up his playing fields, do you? He'll be *cut up* about it!' He chuckled heartily at his hopeless gag. 'Come on, Sara, get picking before Dennis goes even crazier than I am. I've never seen him so keen for anything!'

'I'll pick first,' said Sam. He shoved his finger up his nose and had a good rummage. 'That's better. OK, your turn.'

Sara rolled her eyes but laughed along with the rest of the class. 'I pick Memphis.'

'Big surprise,' grumbled Ruth.

Just as a dark shadow fell without warning over the class, together with a rushing, rustling noise of wings in flight. At least fifty birds were bearing down on them in a solid mass.

'Pigeons!' screamed Ashley, hurling himself to the ground and covering his head.

'Horrible flying rats!' bellowed Ruth, doing the same.

'Bundle!' shouted Smithy, gleefully chucking himself on top of both of them.

A couple more people yelled in alarm, but most were just watching, astounded as the pigeons soared overhead, climbing into the sky.

'It's all right,' Cabbage assured them, blinking up at the crowded sky. 'Perfectly natural. Birds of a feather flock together and all that.'

'Yeah, why turn chicken over a few pigeons?' cried Sam, who seemed fascinated. 'I wonder if they're carrying anything, like the ones in Paris did . . .'

His interest wasn't shared by the rest of the class. 'Run!' squeaked Vicki Starling.

'They'll peck our hair!' shrieked Denise.

'They'll pluck our skirts!' wailed Elise.

'They'll give us nasty little bird fleas!' cried Therese, frowning as her classmates flapped about in panic. 'Won't they?'

'Here they come!' cried Smithy, his head sticking out from beneath a pile of bundling bodies as the pigeons abruptly turned and descended in a slow dive.

Sara clutched hold of Memphis, unsure of what to do. This was like something out of a scary movie. Durbrain was in such a mad panic that he ran slap bang into Cabbage Kale and his bright red umbrella, and all three fell tumbling to the ground.

'Take cover!' yelled Fido, scrambling beneath the stage. 'Remember what happened this morning—they're carrying poo-bombs, and lots of them!'

'OK, I've just turned chicken!' yelled Sam, following Fido's example with a mad squawking noise that helped fuel a fresh surge of panic in the students. They crowded together, desperately trying to fling themselves under the stage. Sara and Memphis cowered under the stack of chairs left at the back of the stage as the birds rushed overhead.

'Get away, you pesky pigeons!' cried Cabbage. He'd picked himself up and was waving his bent and broken brolly at the flock as they started to rise again. 'Go on, flap off! Hop it!'

'Just don't say, "Plop it"!' came Fido's plaintive cry from beneath the stage.

But as it turned out, he didn't need to.

Yells of disgust and alarm went up as the ascending birds unleashed a volley of turds that rained messily down on the stage, the grass, and Cabbage's umbrella. *Please don't hit me!* Sara hoped fervently, tucking her legs in as tightly as she could. *Please, please, please!*

Then, as quickly as it had begun, the dropping of droppings stopped.

A silence fell in the aftermath of the assault. Sara risked peeking out from her hiding place to find the pigeons were retreating now, flying off towards the other side of the school.

'You didn't get me!' yelled Cabbage triumphantly, throwing down his dripping umbrella and shaking an angry fist up at the sky. 'You missed! Missed! Missed!'

At which point, with a wet splat, one last pigeon caught him right on the shoulder.

'Gaaah!' he shouted, jumping around in disgust and rage, much to the amusement of those brave enough to have re-emerged from beneath the stage—Sam amongst them.

'Never mind, sir,' he said, trying to hide a spreading smile. 'Some people say it's lucky!'

'I don't mind!' Cabbage insisted, trying to compose himself and ignore the black and white slug on his shoulder. 'Why should I mind?

It's—it's good for the ground! Yes, a rich fertilizer composed of urates, oxalates, and phosphates . . .'

Fido looked at Sam and smiled. 'That sounds to me like a load of old—!'

'Sir, we must get back inside, quickly!' Vicki urged him. 'What if they come back?'

'They won't come back,' murmured Durbrain. Now he'd crawled back out from under the stage he was staring up at the clouds with a weird smile on his face. 'Show's over.'

'Oh yeah?' Sam challenged. 'And you'd know how a pigeon's mind works, would you?'

'*You* should, Innocent,' Ruth broke in, acting tough again now the birds had flown. 'I've always said you're a bird brain!'

'At least mine's big enough to be classified,' Sam retorted.

'That's enough, you lot,' shouted Cabbage, heading back towards the school. 'Vicki's right, we'll go back inside. I've got some board games, we can play those instead.'

'With creepy accompaniment from whatever's clanking under the floorboards,' Memphis murmured, crawling out from her cover.

'At least that should stop the board games being *bored* games,' joked Sara feebly. But inside, her insides were churning.

Ghosts, thieves, and vengeful pigeons—and it wasn't even Breather yet.

BREATHER

Sam was just getting stuck in to a rousing game of 'rude word' Scrabble against Ashley Lamb when the school hooter's strangulated war-cry brought on Breather. Cabbage was still too busy dabbing at his shoulder with wet paper towels to do much more than grunt goodbye to the class as they filed slowly out of his room.

Normally, everyone fled the classroom to enjoy a few precious moments of freedom in the sunshine. But as the pigeons had just proved, going outside was not without health risks.

'Why have these pigeons got it in for the science department?' Sam wondered, as Sara and Memphis came over to see him. 'Not happy with mucking up the windows, they've started on the teachers.'

'Just coincidence,' said Sara. 'I mean, they can't *know*, can they?'

'Not unless they've been trained, somehow,' said Sam.

'That's impossible,' said Memphis.

'This is Freekham High,' he retorted. 'Nothing's impossible.'

'I just hope getting back those missing costumes isn't impossible,' said Fido, catching the end of their conversation. 'Come on, then— Drama Studio.'

They made their way there, taking care that the skies were clear when crossing from one block to another. But at the Drama Studio, they found that Flange had no good news for them.

'Mr Biggins and I have spent the whole last period searching, but we haven't found a thing,' she said. 'We've looked in the big kitchen bins, searched hedgerows, all the cloakrooms . . .'

'Storerooms?' asked Fido.

'Yes.' Flange ran a hand through her unkempt hair. 'Well, apart from the one in the Humanities Block. Sara and Memphis have already searched there, right?'

Fido turned to Sara and Memphis. 'How well *did* you search before running away?'

'Pretty well,' Sara said defensively. 'But it was dark. The light didn't work.'

Memphis folded her arms. 'Why not go there with Sara right now if you think we missed something.'

Flange shrugged and handed him a set of keys. 'I guess there's nothing to lose.'

'Have you been over to the school farm?' Sam wondered.

'I haven't, but Mr B may have done.'

'Let's check it out anyway,' said Memphis, taking Sam by the arm. 'Come on, you. Later, guys.'

Sam gave a helpless shrug over his shoulder at Sara and Fido as Memphis marched him away. 'What's up, Memphis?'

'Thought you might want to talk,' she said.

'Uh, no, not really,' he told her. 'I actually want to go check up on that pigeon I found.'

'To check it's OK?'

'No, to stamp on it in revenge for what its buddies tried to do to us today,' Sam joked. He checked the sky for any signs of a further attack, but it was blue and clear. 'You don't have to come with.'

'I'm tagging along,' Memphis informed him.

'Sam, I've been watching you today. You've got something on your mind.'

'Boys of my age always have. We learned about it in Personal Health last year.'

'Will you quit with the funny stuff for one moment?'

'It's just that there are so many mysteries today,' Sam complained. 'You know I don't like mysteries. Who nicked the costumes? What's all this about the Freekham ghost? Why have a bunch of pigeons suddenly got it in for the science department?'

Memphis stopped walking and her green eyes bored into his own. 'You're leaving Freekham, aren't you?'

Sam's mouth flapped open and shut in amazement. 'How did you guess?' he spluttered at last.

'I knew it! I just didn't want to believe it.' She sighed. 'You nearly jumped a mile when I talked about you and Sara going your separate ways. You said you won't be sorry to see the last of Penter—oh, just for the summer holidays, of *course*. You—'

'It's heartbreaking for me to learn I'm not as clever as I think I am,' said Sam, 'you know that, right?'

'Why d'you have to go?'

'My dad's almost definitely got a new job and so—'

'—you're moving away,' Memphis concluded, glumly. 'Jeez. You and Sara both.'

Sam's mouth did the flapping thing again. '*What?* Sara's leaving Freekham too?'

'Uh-huh.' Memphis strode off again, dragging him along with her towards the farm. 'Her mum's "almost certainly" got a new job, just like your dad.'

'Figures, I suppose,' he said, with a sad little ache inside. 'We came here together, we leave here together, but . . . well, wasn't she going to tell me?'

Memphis raised an eyebrow. 'Were *you* going to tell *her*?'

'Course I was! Probably. Well, possibly. I mean . . . well . . . maybe after the play.' He sighed. 'I hate goodbyes, see? I've had way above the national average for goodbyes in my life.'

'You two are as bad as each other,' said Memphis. '*I* know why you don't want to tell Sara. You're worried she won't be as upset about it as you are.'

87

'Yeah, right,' Sam blustered. 'As if!'

'And it's exactly the same reason why she doesn't want to tell you,' sighed Memphis. 'Well, personally, I'm going to miss you both.' She glanced at him as they walked, her green eyes cool and appraising as ever. 'You two are Knot and Innocent—together, you're *Not Innocent*! You're Sam and Sara—but put together you make *Samsara*—'

Sam groaned. 'Here comes the mad mystic stuff again!'

'My mum's a Buddhist, what can I say! Samsara is their word for the endless cycle of birth and rebirth. Don't you get it?'

Sam nodded. 'I get that you are a nut.'

'It was, like, your destiny to come here! Freakiness is re-enacted here at Freekham again and again—and you two seem to be the latest triggers.' Memphis sighed. 'Wonder what'll happen once you're gone?'

'Bit of peace and quiet, maybe,' Sam suggested. 'For everyone!'

They walked along in silence for a while.

'Memphis, you won't tell Sara I'm going, will you?'

'I won't. But *you* should.' She half-smiled. 'And if Sara does decide to tell you that she's out of here, don't let on I already told you, 'K?'

''K,' Sam agreed.

They had reached the school farm—and much to Sam's surprise, Daisy Pellock was just closing the gate to the grounds, on her way out. She was carrying a big, old-fashioned metal lunch box in one hand, and she didn't look pleased to see them.

'Hi,' said Sam. 'Great minds think alike, huh?'

'Huh?' Daisy echoed.

'Well, didn't you come here to check up on that pigeon?'

'Er . . . yeah,' she admitted. 'It's fine now. Back in the loft.'

Sam nodded down the path to the main farm building. 'Is Pacemaker there?'

'He was. But he's just gone into a meeting.'

'Who with?'

Daisy shrugged and swung the lunch box behind her back.

Sam noticed and smiled. 'Can't wait till lunchtime, huh? I have days like that too.'

Daisy gave him a look that was pure ice. 'You

don't know what you're talking about,' she hissed, and pushed past him.

Sam watched her go. 'What did I say?'

'I've heard she's been a bit jittery lately,' said Memphis. 'Troubles at home. Her dad's a builder and he's been out of work for ages. They'll have to sell their house if he can't get a job soon.' She shrugged. 'Must be tough. I'm not surprised she's turned to a bit of comfort eating.'

'I guess,' said Sam, watching her vanish into the crowd of people on their way to their next classes.

As Sara led Fido to the Humanities storeroom, the reek of chemicals grew ever stronger. It took her a while to notice. She was wondering about Sam. There was definitely something on his mind, and had been all day.

Sara wondered how he'd take it if he knew she was going. It wasn't as if she wanted him to burst into tears or tell her he couldn't struggle on without her—that would be creepy and gross—but she wanted him to at least care she was leaving. Trouble was, with boys like Sam it was hard to know *what* they cared about. The only thing he took seriously was his next joke.

'Whoa, Sara,' called Fido. As he grabbed her by the shirt-sleeve, she suddenly realized she was sailing straight past the storeroom. 'This is the place, remember? So which key is it?'

Sara hunted through the keys. 'Er . . . this one, I think.'

'What a stink,' said Fido, sticking the key in the lock. 'If there really is a Freekham ghost, it can't have a nose . . .' He tailed off, frowning.

'What is it?'

'This door,' he said. 'It was already unlocked.'

Then a creepy, bloodcurdling wail started up from inside the storeroom, louder than ever before.

'Oh my God!' cried Sara, backing away. 'You see? It's in there! It's in there!'

'I wish I had my camcorder on me,' muttered Fido. Bravely, he flung open the door.

The storeroom seemed empty, save for the sharp stink of chemicals.

'Who's in there?' Fido called, trying to keep his voice steady.

Sara felt the hairs on the back of her neck stand up on end as a low, menacing chuckle started up. Then, in the gloomy light spilling in from the corridor, she caught a glimpse of movement at the back of the storeroom. 'I saw something!' she cried.

Fido grabbed a mop from beside the doorway and hurled it like a javelin into the shadows.

He was rewarded by a shout of pain and some very loud swearing.

'Ha!' cried Fido. 'If that's a ghost, I'm a monkey's second cousin.'

'I had my suspicions,' Sara told him. Then she pushed him aside, angry that she had ever been fooled. 'Who's in there? Come out, you freak!'

'All right,' came a familiar voice. 'But no more mops!'

Sara and Fido stared at each other in disbelief. 'Durbrain!'

'Yeah, me,' said Durbrain, rubbing his stomach where the mop had spiked him, and holding his nose with his other hand. 'So what?'

'So *you're* the Freekham ghost,' said Fido. 'Or the Freekham fraud, more like.'

'I don't get it,' said Sara. 'You've been telling everyone in school there's no such thing as the Freekham ghost—and yet it's you all the time?'

'Never heard of the double bluff?' Durbrain gave her a dopey smile. 'It was all a brilliant hoax by me. I made spooky recordings and left them playing in secret places around the school.' He pointed to a dusty tape recorder on a shelf. 'But this storeroom is the easiest to get into, so I made it my base of scary operations!'

'How come you've been able to get in here?' Sara demanded.

Durbrain shrugged. 'Stole one of Biggins's spare keys. It's been such a laugh, tricking so many stupid idiots into thinking ghosts really exist.'

'Takes a stupid idiot to know one.' Sara stood there seething. 'And just how did you make the clanking noise?'

'Er . . .' Durbrain seemed to need to think about that. 'Er . . . Cabbage was right. That was a dodgy boiler playing up—the sound carries through the hot-water pipes.'

'Lucky for you.' Sara took a deep, calming breath. 'Where did that mop go, Fido?'

'At the back somewhere I guess. Why?'

She advanced on the dopey, curly-haired faker. 'Because it's my turn to clobber Durbrain with it!'

93

'No!' he cried, backing away rapidly. 'Stay back! Stay—*WHOA*!'

Sara saw him stumble over something and topple backwards. With a clang and a squawk, he banged his head on the filing cabinet at the back of the room—and fell on something soft.

'Look!' gasped Fido. He rolled Durbrain aside, then pulled out a long red robe. 'It's the monk costume!'

Sara frowned. 'You're kidding.'

'I'm not! Look, here are the others!' Fido whooped for joy as he grabbed hold of the costumes and draped them over Sara's outstretched arms. 'They were all just dumped here on the floor!'

'Brilliant!' grinned Sara, clutching them to her chest. 'I must have missed them before.'

'Or they've been dumped here since,' said Fido. 'Who cares? Well done, Durbrain! We owe it all to you.'

'And for that, I *won't* sock you with the mop after all,' Sara told him sweetly. 'What did you trip over, anyway?'

'Nothing,' said Durbrain.

Fido snatched it up from the ground. 'Some

battered old metal thing—sort of a lunch box.'

'I'm sure that wasn't here before,' said Sara.

'Looks like it's been here forever if you ask me.' Fido dumped it back on the floor. 'Unlucky for you, Durbrain. But lucky for us!'

'Bet you'll tell everyone the ghost is just a hoax, now, won't you?' moaned Durbrain.

'Duh! Course we will!' Fido agreed cheerily. 'And I hope everyone you've scared comes after you with something bigger and blunter than a mop!'

'Hang on,' said Durbrain. 'I'm lying on something else here. Ow! What is it?'

'If it's pea-sized and wet, it's your brain,' said Fido.

'It's worth a lot more than that, I reckon!' Durbrain held out an oversized golden golfball.

Sara snatched it from his fat fingers. 'Awarded to Freekham High School, Teachers Golfing Association,' she read. 'First prize.' She stared at Fido. 'It must be the Head's! This must be one of the valuables Penter said was nicked from the Head's office!'

'It's only gold-plated,' said Fido. 'Can't be worth much.'

'Probably why the thief dumped it,' said Sara.

'There's a fountain pen here too,' Durbrain announced. 'Looks flash.'

'Give me a biro any day,' said Fido.

'Ain't got one,' said Durbrain.

Fido sighed and slipped the pen and the paperweight into his pocket.

'We'd better tell Flange and let her hand these back to the Head,' said Sara. 'We don't want anyone thinking *we* nicked them.'

Fido nodded. 'Anything else down there, Durbrain?'

'Don't think so.'

'Then thank you, and goodnight.' With that, Fido slammed the door on him, turned and set off with a spring in his step back down towards the Drama Studio. Sara struggled after him with the heavy costumes, a big bundle of red.

'So, Durbrain is the school ghost,' she said. 'But we still don't know who the thief is, why they took all the costumes—and why they bothered to nick those rubbishy things from the Head's office.'

Fido shrugged. 'Oh, well. What matters is, we've got the outfits back for the dress rehearsal. Hopefully Flange will get us off Computer

Studies so we can check they're OK and sort them out ready for lunchtime.'

As they hurried into the corridor that led to the Drama Studio, they almost sent Daisy Pellock flying. She recoiled, holding up both hands as if trying to ward them away.

'Hey, Daisy!' Fido grinned. 'We found the costumes, look! Isn't that fantastic?'

'Oh.' For a few moments Daisy looked perplexed. 'Oh, right, yeah. That's fantastic. Nice one.'

Fido gave her a funny look. 'Your enthusiasm is overwhelming. Come on, *chief* costume designer, I need you to check them over. Ask Flange, she'll get you out of next lesson.'

'Sorry,' she said. 'Stuff I need to do.' Then the school hooter sounded its mad, grunting squeal to usher in the start of period five. Daisy looked down at the ground and pushed quickly past them. 'Gotta go,' she called back over her shoulder. 'I'll check them later, yeah?'

'Daisy!' called Sara. 'Is anything wrong?'

'Wrong? With me? Nah. I'm just . . . I'm probably just hungry, that's all.' She gave a helpless kind of smile and vanished around the corner.

'Maybe we should have brought along that big old lunch box from the storeroom,' said Fido. 'Might have had some hundred-year-old sandwiches inside it!'

'Yeah,' said Sara. 'Maybe.' To be honest, food was about the last thing on her mind, what with the under-rehearsed play looming ever-closer and a possibly painful convo with Sam to get through . . .

And the craziest feeling that something big was waiting to happen on this last day at Freekham High.

Periods Five and Six
Double Computer Studies

Sam and Memphis were first into the computer lab, and slumped down in their respective places. Teetering in his chair, casting a long shadow against the bright white walls, Sam was trying to work out what he would say to Sara when she came in.

Then Fido dashed inside, beaming all over his face, and Sam got his answer. 'Me and Sara aren't coming to this lesson.'

Sam wasn't sure whether to feel disappointed or relieved. 'Are you here by mistake, then?'

'I'm only here to get out of *being* here.' He waved a note under Sam's nose. 'Letter from Flange. She's letting us do a technical run—so Sara's doing a full read-through with scenery in place for the first time—and get this!' He grinned across at Memphis. 'We found the costumes. *And* we found the Freekham ghost!'

Sam and Memphis did a double-take—or rather, a *double* double-take, since there were two of them. 'Huh?'

Fido was enjoying the moment. '*Uh*-huh. We found out who's been staging the whole thing.'

'I knew it couldn't be real!' said Sam. 'Then who—?'

'I don't believe it, Durbrain!' bellowed Ruth Cook. 'It was you all the time?' She marched inside at the head of a small but angry mob, holding the big boy's arm behind his back. 'Trying to make a fool of us, was you?'

'I was just mucking about!' Durbrain protested.

Vicki Starling jabbed a finger into his chest. 'I almost smeared my make-up when I heard those clanging noises in the girls' loos!' Her chic clique sighed in sympathy.

Ashley pushed forwards and scowled at him. 'And you ruined a really good debate on Wednesday, making those stupid noises.'

Durbrain looked baffled for a moment. 'Oh, yeah, the storeroom's just the other side of the debating chamber, isn't it? Sorry.' He winced as Ruth's grip on his arm tightened.

100

'Ashley said the debate was after school,' Sam realized. 'If you didn't know the storeroom was next to the debating chamber, why did you stay?'

'I *did* know,' Durbrain argued. 'I—I just forgot for a minute.'

Memphis had stood up at the back of the class. 'But me and Sara heard the ghost this morning—and you were still in the Drama Studio, then.'

'He used tape recorders,' Fido explained, keen to grab back some glory of discovery.

'You went to a lot of trouble,' Sam noted.

'And now he's *in* a lot of trouble,' hissed Ruth.

'So what was in it for you?' asked Memphis. 'You must have known people would be mad at you once they knew.'

'They shouldn't have found out. But Fido and Sara surprised me in the storeroom at Breather,' said Durbrain. 'Figured I should 'fess up myself before they told everyone.'

'Didn't waste much time, did you?' said Sam. 'Almost like you suddenly decided you *wanted* people to know.'

Durbrain frowned. 'Yeah, well—'

But just then, Mr 'Gricey' Grice the Computer

Studies teacher came inside. He was shabbily dressed, with a shiny pink head and a moustache so sharp and bristly you could strip paint with it. 'What's going on here? End of term high spirits?'

Ruth gave Durbrain's arm a final twist before letting him go. 'More like low-down *fake* spirits,' she muttered.

'Well, break it up, all of you,' said Gricey sternly. 'Take your seats. If you muck around, I won't let you play my summer quiz.'

Sam slumped into his seat and glanced at Michelle Harris behind him. 'And that *would* be devastating, wouldn't it?'

'Sorry, sir, I've got to run,' said Fido, producing his note. 'And Sara Knot already has. It's the school play, you know.'

'We teachers are really looking forward to this play,' said Gricey. 'Once we've struggled through the Head's farewell lunch for Mr Collier, of course.' He cleared his throat, perhaps aware he'd said too much. 'Anyway, thank you, Fido. Off you go.'

Fido sprinted from the room, and Gricey got up. 'Right, I'm going to put you in teams of four.

I want each team to pick a subject, research it online, then prepare five questions on that subject to ask your opposing teams.'

'Is there a prize for the team who comes first?' asked Smithy hopefully.

'There's a big slab of fig and hazelnut flapjack baked by my wife!'

'In other words, no, there *isn't* a prize,' sighed Sam.

Gricey divided the room up into teams. Sam found himself partnered with Michelle, Therese, and Ginger Mutton.

'What subject shall we choose?' wondered Ginger, nudging her chunky glasses back up her freckled nose. 'How about sock darning through the ages?'

'How about, "Put a sock in it"!' said Sam.

'Hairspray?' ventured Therese.

Michelle shrugged. 'Tropical fish?'

'Pigeons!' Sam declared. All three girls shrank back in disgust. 'Go on, let's look up some pigeons—far safer than looking up *at* them.' He smiled. 'I'd like to know how pigeons can be trained, and if synchronized dropping of droppings is common. *And* I want to know what those little letters and numbers on homing pigeons' tags mean.'

The girls looked at him doubtfully.

'And I'll do all the work,' he added.

'Dunno about you two, but I think pigeons is a great idea!' Ginger smiled. 'Sam, you just got yourself a deal.'

Sara was getting totally bored with the journey between the Drama Studio and the storeroom in the Humanities Block. She'd just run through the whole play with Fido, Flange, and the guys from the year above who were supervising the sets. As she narrated the passing centuries, they shifted the relevant bits of scenery in and out of view—only the painted brick wall, daubed with Durbrain's bright red splodges, remained constant at the back of the stage.

It had all gone quite smoothly, considering the frantic rush. But now Fido was throwing a fit because a few accessories were missing from the blokes' costumes—two medals from a soldier's uniform, a bow tie, and a schoolboy cap. To calm him down, Sara had offered to go and check the storeroom yet again.

Sara turned up her nose as the whiff of chemicals carried to her once more. There was the storeroom, still flanked by its evacuated classrooms. But the stink didn't seem as bad as before. And at least, now Durbrain had revealed himself to be the school ghost, there was nothing to—

She heard laughter. Muffled, low laughter. Where was it coming from?

The *storeroom*?

A shiver of fear went through Sara. No, she told herself, the sound must have come from one of the classrooms. She flipped up the sign on the door on the left and looked inside. No, it was empty. Same story with the room on the right.

Then she caught movement way off to her left. A man in an apron was wheeling along a trolley full of sandwiches. He turned out of sight.

Curious, Sara followed the man down a corridor that ran at right angles to the main thoroughfare. She realized it led round to the debating chamber, a relic of the original Freekham Grammar School that stood here before the German bombs fell. The laughter grew louder, and Sara peered inside. Several kitchen staff were milling about the grand table in the centre of the room, laying place settings.

'Put the sarnies down there, Joe,' one large, forbidding woman called over. 'Hope the bread's good and soft. We don't want poor old Collier's false teeth falling out!'

The others cackled and hooted. 'Might not be such a bad idea,' another woman suggested, swaying as if she'd had one nip too many from the cooking sherry. 'They can send *him* off to retirement, but hang on to his dentures!'

There was more laughter, as if this was the most hilarious thing ever. Sara crept away back along the corridor. So this was where they were holding the farewell meal for Killer Collier—the oldest part of the school, for the oldest teacher in the school. Decades of loyal service, then booted out with a few sarnies in his belly. It was kind of sad.

And yet, as she thought about it, she found she couldn't stop giggling. By the time she had reached the storeroom, she was openly laughing. She felt quite dizzy.

Then, as she put the key in the lock, she froze.

There was the muffled laughter again. Must be one of Durbrain's tapes. She would turn it off. The idea made her chuckle.

She threw open the door—but then jumped as the heavy wood smacked against something. There was a shout of pain.

It was Penter! He'd come up beside her and she'd whacked the door into his head!

Sara bit her lip as she watched him reeling about the corridor. She should have been terrified of the consequences. Instead, she had to fight to keep a straight face. He looked ridiculous, jumping about and holding his nose.

'Knot, what on earth do you think you're doing?' he demanded crossly, finally coming to a halt.

'Looking for something from the storeroom, sir,' she told him, digging her nails into her palms to stop herself laughing. 'I've got Flange's permission, sir.'

Penter frowned. '*Mrs* Flange, you mean.'

'Yeah. Her.' Sara could feel the laughter bubbling up. *Get a grip!* she told herself fiercely. *What's the matter with you?* 'Did you want something, sir?'

'Yes, less cheek from you, girl!' Penter said gravely. 'I am here to check that everything is prepared for Mr Collier's farewell luncheon.'

'They're working on it now,' said Sara. 'It was good that the costumes turned up again, wasn't it, sir? And the Head's . . . er . . . valuables.'

'That miserable thief clearly had a change of heart,' Penter agreed, 'as well as costume.'

Sara snorted with mirth. Then she clamped her hand over her mouth and staggered into the storeroom hoping he wouldn't see her laughing. She felt really dizzy . . .

'Whatever's the matter with you, girl?' asked Penter, starting forwards.

'Nothing, sir.' She opened the drawer of the filing cabinet and rummaged about inside for the missing accessories. 'Sir, can you see a bow cap anywhere? And a schoolboy medal. And some ties? No, that came out wrong. A schoolboy's tie . . . A soldier's bow . . .'

Suddenly, Penter started giggling too. Sara turned round, stunned into silence. He rarely so much as tittered, and yet here he was, shaking with laughter as he peered first into the storeroom, then into the classrooms either side of it.

'I say, how funny,' he remarked, baring his big yellow teeth in a gormless grin, 'the storeroom isn't long enough.'

Sara blinked. 'What?'

'Look at its depth, compared to the depth of the classroom beside it. It should go back a lot further.'

'Oh.' She tapped on the wall behind the filing cabinet. 'Well, it doesn't.'

'Oh.' He giggled again. 'How silly.'

'Hey, Mr Hayes told us that this block was built around the ruins of the old science block.' Sara grinned. 'Maybe there's a bit of old brick-work behind here.'

'That's a good possibility,' said Penter. He shook his head as if trying to clear it. 'I'm glad to hear you're paying attention to your teachers. Now, hurry along back to Mrs Flange, Knot.' He took a step backwards, and walked unsteadily away. 'I'm really feeling quite peculiar . . .'

'I know the feeling,' muttered Sara. Her head was beginning to pound as she crouched on the floor to search for the missing accessories. Her hands soon closed on something soft. It was the red schoolboy cap, and the scarlet bow tie was stuffed inside it. She groped around for the medals, but there was nothing else—

Her hands suddenly chanced upon something hard, square, and metal. The old lunch box. Curious, Sara opened the catches, and found a sandwich, an apple, and a small flask. She opened it and sniffed the sickly-smelling fruity drink inside. The apple was perfectly fresh. This was a new lunch, not a hundred-year-old one.

Sara straightened up, and another wave of dizziness broke over her. She supposed the lunch box must be Durbrain's. And yet, why had he just left it there?

Suddenly she heard a loud, grating rattle, close by in the gloom. She paused, wondering whether to crack up laughing or simply accept she was cracking up.

Then, with some relief, she noticed a dusty old tape recorder on the middle shelf. Durbrain said he had made a scary recording—the machine wasn't playing, but as she ejected the tape inside she saw it had reached its end. Maybe it had just finished playing?

Clutching it tightly, she listened carefully. No more laughter. Just silence.

After a while in the gloom, Sara found she could hear little other than the pounding in her head. She hadn't found the medals, but who really cared? She slipped the tape in her pocket, tottered out of the storeroom and locked the door behind her. The corridor was sunlit, the jollity of the distant dinner ladies reassuring—as if this was reality, and the storeroom was somewhere else. Even her head was starting to clear a bit.

As Sara made her way back to the Drama Studio, she decided she would never go back to that storeroom, ever again.

Sam stared at the links page on the computer screen, engrossed in the weird and wacky world of pigeons he had uncovered. Pigeons were way older than humans—they had been around for more than thirty million years. They had been used to carry messages as early as the twelfth century. Mighty warlord Ghengis Khan swore by them.

And the trusty birds had served in several wars. Some of them had even won medals! As recently as 2002, there was a trained pigeon police service in remote parts of India—the birds could deliver messages in case of natural disasters wiping out communications.

Sam learned that pigeons were able to steer so accurately because they had some kind of natural built-in compass. They used the position of the sun and the stars to fix their own position—but only at first. Scientists had found out that the birds also had a kind of satellite navigation system built in! If they made the same journey several times, they noted the landmarks below—like a major road or a railway track. And to save them the bother of working out where the sun was and which was the quickest way home, they simply followed those landmarks because they knew it would lead them back to their lofts in the end—flying round roundabouts and taking the proper junctions and everything! There was something both extremely clever and very lazy about that which Sam totally admired. He decided there and then that pigeons were cool.

And he learned about the little bands they wore around their legs. Fitted at birth, they would stay on a racing pigeon for its whole life—and contained information that could identify them if they got lost. The letters at the start of the tag stood for a particular pigeon club. The next two numbers were the year it was born, and the ones after that made up the pigeon's special identity code. Sam supposed that was more thorough than simply naming it Nigel and adding the owner's phone number.

So, what did the code on the pigeon he'd discovered stand for? What *was* the MVPA?

'Haven't you come up with five questions yet?' grumbled Ginger.

'Here's five fingers,' he retorted, holding up a hand for her to talk to.

He typed in the code and waited to see what the search engine came up with.

MVPA
Madagascar Veterans Pigeon
Association
Chairman: Major Quentin
Pacemaker (Retired)

'Well, well,' murmured Sam. 'That pigeon wasn't one of Ferret's—it was one of *Pacemaker's.*

And Collier must have known it was. So why did he lie to me?'

Michelle made him jump by tapping him on the shoulder. 'Sam, why are you talking to yourself?'

'Um . . . Well, I wasn't really *talking* . . .'

But for all his mumbling and stumbling over words, the answer was obvious to Sam.

He was talking to himself because Sara wasn't here.

I am going to miss that girl, he thought.

'I was just working out the last of my questions,' he told Ginger finally—and just in time.

'All right!' Gricey clapped his hands. 'Let the mega-quiz commence! Sam, your team first, I think. Set your questions to Elise's team.'

Sam studied his opponents. Elise had a confident smile on her prim and pretty face. Her teammates Ashley and Denise sat either side, bright-eyed and eager. Durbrain was slumped beside Ashley, the living definition of 'bored stupid'.

'The subject is pigeons,' Sam announced. Elise and Denise groaned in perfect unison, and Ashley turned up his nose. But Durbrain suddenly sat up straight.

'Question one. When did the British armed forces decide that pigeons were of no further use in war?'

Elise stared coldly at him. '*What?*'

'How are we meant to know that!' protested Denise.

'1948,' said Durbrain.

Everyone in the whole class stared at him.

'Is the right answer,' said Sam slowly. 'OK, question two. What's another name for the little band around a pigeon's leg?'

Durbrain answered without hesitation: 'A ring.'

'Correct.' Sam paused while the class broke out in astonished gasps.

'I told you we should have gone for sock darning through the ages,' hissed Ginger.

Sam sighed and ignored her. 'If you happen to find a lost homing pigeon, what should you feed it?'

'Wild bird seed and unpopped popcorn is good,' said Durbrain. 'But if you give them water, make sure it's in a bowl that's a few centimetres deep. Most birds scoop up water, but not pigeons. They stick their whole beak in the water and drink it down that way.'

Gricey looked taken aback. 'I think you deserve a bonus point for that answer, Dennis.'

Sam's eyes narrowed. Clearly he'd picked the one subject Durbrain knew something about. So it was time to change the line of questioning.

'Right,' he said. 'Can pigeons be trained to perform certain actions when they're given a special signal?'

'Yeah, course,' said Durbrain.

'And last question,' Sam rattled off quickly, 'could *you* train them?'

'Yeah,' he blurted, 'easy, I've done it loads of—'

He broke off, but too late. *Gotcha*, thought Sam with satisfaction.

Durbrain frowned and went bright red. 'What kind of a question was that, Innocent?'

'I'm afraid I have to ask the same thing, Sam,' said Gricey, wagging a finger.

'It was probably a stupid question,' Sam admitted, shooting a long, cool look at Durbrain. *But it got a very interesting answer*, he thought.

'How do you know so much about pigeons?' asked Ashley, half admiring and half resentful.

Durbrain shrugged. 'My dad keeps racing pigeons.'

'Has he beaten one yet?' Sam joked.

'He's been teaching me all about them,' Durbrain went on over the resultant sniggers. 'I've seen pigeons do some amazing things.' He smiled. 'But I don't reckon anyone's seen *anything* like what those pigeons did out in the fields today.'

You know loads more than you're saying, Sam decided. *But what?*

'Thank you, Sam's team,' said Gricey. 'But I'm afraid you haven't done very well. At the end of your round, Elise's team have got six out of five! A tough act to follow . . .'

That proved to be the case. Durbrain's incredible performance in the first few minutes made his team the overall winner. But since that meant they were lumbered with an all-too-generous portion of fig and hazelnut flapjack, Elise and the others weren't exactly overjoyed.

The hooter finally called time on the lesson. Lunchtime at last, thought Sam, amid the scrape of chairs and the clatter of eager footsteps on the tiled floor. Time for the dress rehearsal in the

117

Drama Studio—and to tell Sara what he had learned.

'Who would believe that Durbrain actually *knew* stuff!' said Michelle, still marvelling.

'Only stuff about pigeons,' Ginger pointed out.

'He really is an expert though, isn't he?' said Sam. 'Which, if you ask me, is very interesting.'

From the blank looks on the girls' faces, and the speed with which they left the classroom, they *weren't* asking him.

LUNCHTIME

When Sara got back to the Drama Studio, she found it empty save for Daisy sorting through the big pile of costumes, without much enthusiasm.

'Fido and Flange around?' Sara asked.

'They've gone to the playing fields to start setting up the stage,' said Daisy, without looking up.

'I hope they're going to give it a good hose down after what those flying rats did to it.' Sara shuddered.

Daisy didn't react. 'They'll be back for dress rehearsal at half-past.'

'I've found the missing accessories Fido was after,' Sara said, waving the cap and bow tie. 'Well, most of them. No sign of the medals.'

'Didn't think there would be,' said Daisy quietly. She wiped at her cheeks, and suddenly Sara could see the wetness there.

'You're crying!' Sara sat down beside her. 'What's wrong?'

'Nothing,' said Daisy, sniffing miserably and staring at the floor.

'Some nothings don't always seem so bad if you talk about them.'

Daisy looked up at Sara, her eyes big, wet, and worried, her lip trembling. 'Oh God, Sara, I'm in trouble. I should never have got involved in it, but . . .'

'Involved in what?' Sara asked gently.

Daisy looked back down at the pile of costumes, wiped her eyes on her sleeve.

'*What*, Daisy?'

'Duh!' she said suddenly. 'This play, of course!'

Sara looked at her doubtfully. 'Daisy, you seem kind of upset—'

'I was supposed to check everyone was happy with the costume adjustments this morning,' she said, wiping crossly at the tears she couldn't seem to stop. 'Now it's almost the dress rehearsal and I *still* haven't done it.'

Sara sighed. 'I can't help you out if you won't let me.'

'There's nothing you can do,' said Daisy.

That seemed to be that, so Sara got back up and wandered over to a corner to go over her lines once again. The other actors would be here soon, ready for the dress rehearsal, Sam included. She felt as if she'd hardly seen him all day. And she was running out of opportunities . . . Of course, having a serious talk while he was wearing a monk's habit would be kind of weird . . .

But since when had weird ever stopped them?

In the corner, she noticed a tape recorder for playing in sound effects and things. To put her mind at rest about what she had heard back in the storeroom, Sara decided to play Durbrain's ghostly tape. She slotted it in and hit the rewind. Pressed play. Nothing. Rewound a little further. Pressed play again. Nothing. Left it rewinding for a while. Hit play.

'Bonjour, Madame! On peut manger ceci sans dangeur? Pourquoi l'eau est-elle brune?'

Sara frowned to hear the woman's cheery French gobbledegook. It sounded like some kind of lesson on tape—pretty scary in itself, but certainly not a home-made ghostly recording. Alarmed, she rewound some more—still French, a bloke this time, asking if he could buy bicycles for his pet dog or something. Again and again, she rewound and played and caught several snatches of *le beau Français*—but there was not a ghostly wail or chuckle to be had.

She'd taken this tape from the recorder in the storeroom. And judging by the dust on the machine, it hadn't been disturbed in some time. If Durbrain *had* made a tape, this wasn't it. And it hadn't been played on that recorder.

A shiver went through her. So what *had* she heard? If Durbrain wasn't the ghost . . . who was?

Sam grabbed himself a cheese roll from the canteen, told Memphis he'd see her at the dress rehearsal, and made his way over to the school farm. Maybe he should have asked her to come with him, he thought. Then again, commando-style missions were best performed solo . . .

His head was full of questions and he wanted some answers.

Like, why were there so many pigeons around the school all of a sudden? Why were they racing about on these search-and-poop missions—coincidence or careful training? Durbrain seemed to have the knowhow—but what was the motive?

It seemed likely that Pacemaker was involved too. He had brought at least one of his own pigeons along to Freekham High—did he have others? Did all the pigeons who'd been attacking Penter's windows belong to him? Why pick on *those* windows?

One possibility occurred to Sam as he moved through the straggles of students along the pathway. His form room had the only clear view of the farm. What if somebody needed that view covered up from time to time, so they could do something dodgy. Something in secret . . .

The farm itself seemed deserted. Sam slipped through the gates and jogged up to the main doors. They were locked. He squinted through the glass panel for signs of life inside. There was movement in one of the classrooms. It looked like Durbrain, talking to someone.

'Well, well,' muttered Sam. He had to find another way inside. He needed to hear what Durbrain was saying . . .

So Sam started to case the joint. He skulked

round to the right, and soon saw something weird peeping round the far side of the farm block—it looked a bit like a scrappy garden shed. Avian coos and ruffling noises came from within.

'A makeshift pigeon loft, built on to the old one,' Sam realized, with growing excitement. 'They've built an extension for Pacemaker's pigeons!'

He started towards it, crouching down so no one could see him through the windows. But the school goat could see him, and it bleated loudly, again and again.

'Just my luck—a guard goat!' Sam quickly retreated back round to the front and decided to try the left hand side of the building.

Aha—this was more like it. Although the blinds were still down in Ferret's office, the window was partly open. Sam listened, but couldn't hear anyone inside. So carefully but quickly, he scrambled inside.

And felt a chill go through him.

This was no longer a teacher's office. It was a war room. A large aerial view of the school was pinned to one wall, divided into grids—clearly it had been enlarged from the one he'd found outside. A large green rectangle marked Penter's windows, and red circles were daubed over the playing fields. Little dotted paths were marked all over it—pigeon flight paths perhaps?

There were diagrams of pigeons and old black-and-white photos of soldiers in the jungle and blurry shots of explosions going off.

Most sinister of all, a picture of the headmaster was taped to the door with a big felt-tipped red circle over his face. PRIME TARGET FOR OBLITERATION was written in big scrawly capitals above his head.

'What the hell is Ferret up to?' breathed Sam.

Just as the door swung open to reveal Pacemaker, Durbrain—and Killer Collier.

'Mr Ferret is not up to anything, boy,' said Collier quietly. '*We* are.'

Sam gulped. He guessed he was in deep trouble.

'Should have kept your stupid nose out, Innocent,' said Durbrain. 'Now you're for it.'

'For what?' He looked at Collier innocently. ''Scuse me, sir, but shouldn't you be at your farewell lunch?'

'Don't be ludicrous, boy!' snapped Pacemaker. 'It doesn't officially begin for another thirteen minutes!'

'Farewell lunch,' Collier scoffed. 'This is not a farewell, it's *goodbye*. A final goodbye—no going back.'

'Bye then,' said Sam. He made a dash for the window, but Durbrain grabbed hold of him and yanked him back.

Pacemaker marched stiffly over to the window and closed it. Then he wedged his monocle into place and scrutinized Sam. 'It appears there is a spy in our midst, gentlemen!'

'I'm not a spy,' said Sam. 'I'm just confused. I know you're *Major* Pacemaker, the head of the Madagascar Veterans Pigeon Association and I know Durbrain can train pigeons—'

Durbrain scowled. 'You tricked that info out of me!'

'Yeah, it's a neat little con, it's called "asking a question",' said Sam. 'You should ask yourself—what exactly have you got into?'

'Why?'

'Because I want to know the answer!'

'It sounds as if you know a good deal already,'

said Pacemaker, ominously. 'Enough to incrimi-nate us.'

'So you may as well tell me some more! I mean, if I like the sound of what you're doing . . . Maybe we could join forces?'

Pacemaker's bristly moustache twitched. 'Eh?'

'It's my last day here at Freekham,' Sam went on. 'Be nice to go out on a high. So come on. Pigeons are the link between you and Durbrain—er, Dennis. But how?'

'Young Durban here is a remarkable talent,' said Pacemaker. 'He's certainly taught a couple of old war-horses some new tricks.'

'I thought he was training pigeons, not war-horses?'

'Idiot boy!' cried Pacemaker. 'I mean that after sixty years' experience, we thought we knew the bally lot about birds. But young Durban here has taught *us* a few things about how to train pigeons.' He guffawed. 'Yes, I've been following his progress with interest these past two years. He's quite notorious on the pigeon fanciers' circuit.'

Sam raised an eyebrow. 'You fancy pigeons?'

'Ha, ha.' Durbrain glowered at him. 'It's what they call people who are into racing pigeons.'

'And this is how you got your coursework re-graded by Mr Collier,' Sam realized. 'You've sold him your services!'

'Fair enough, isn't it?' said Durbrain. 'I do something for him, he does something for me.'

'But what?' Sam looked at Killer, who was looking sort-of shamefaced at the floor. 'Sir, what *has* he done for you?'

'I've given the best years of my life to this school,' said Killer quietly. 'Decade after decade.'

'And how do they reward his loyalty?' squawked Pacemaker. 'At the first sign of an off-day, the headmaster kicks him out! Forces him into . . . *retirement*.' He spoke the word as if it tasted of wee. 'Well, it's not on, is it?' He turned to Collier and clapped him on the back. A little cloud of chalk dust rose up from the old boy's pinstripes. 'I said to Lionel, I said: Lionel, this headmaster needs to be taught a lesson! You're a soldier, man! You must fight back! You leave it to me—I'll mastermind the whole thing . . . Don't end your last day with a whimper— go out with a bang!'

It's my last day too, thought Sam miserably. *Forget bangs! Whimpers are cool! I love whimpers!* If only he *had* told Memphis where he was going . . .

He found himself staring at the red circles on the Head's head and on the map of the school and its grounds—and finally understood. 'Of course!' he breathed. 'The Head will be on stage this afternoon for the full school assembly—and *he's* the target for all the pigeons you've brought here, isn't he?'

Durbrain giggled.

'You're using colours and shapes to give them a focus,' Sam realized. 'In the quiz I asked you if pigeons could be trained to behave in certain ways using triggers—and you didn't hesitate, did you? In period four, Cabbage Kale was carrying a big red umbrella—to any pigeons overhead it would have looked like a big red circle!'

'Stupid idiot, carrying an umbrella on a hot day,' grumbled Durbrain. 'And it *would* happen just when Mr Pacemaker was letting out the pigeons for a test flight.'

'No wonder you kept trying to get Cabbage to put the umbrella down.'

'As it happened, the whole affair was rather a

stroke of luck,' Pacemaker chuckled. 'Proves that the stunt will work this afternoon.'

Durbrain smiled. 'I've painted red circles all over the big board they're sticking up at the back of the stage, and there's loads of red in the costumes. I've trained the pigeons so that when they *see* all that red, they'll dive down and get busy. And the brightest ones will even recognize the Head's face from his photograph,' he added proudly. 'When they spy him sitting there, they'll zero in and—'

'Bombs away,' Sam muttered. 'Like with Penter's windows.'

'Yes, their droppings have made an effective smokescreen,' Collier chuckled. 'Mr Pacemaker, as you may have guessed, is not a supply teacher. He has no right to be here at all.'

'But I have every right to take revenge on the silly asses who pick a fight with one of my men!' roared Pacemaker, his left eye twitching fiercely.

'We didn't want people to see him coming and going from here too often,' Killer went on. 'Since Mr Ferret is . . . er . . . *away*, the school farm is officially closed.'

Sam's eyes widened. 'What have you done with him?'

'He's perfectly well,' said Collier.

'Of course he is!' roared Pacemaker. 'Taken care of very nicely!'

Sam began to wonder just how 'nicely' he was going to be taken care of by this crew of loonies. *Keep them talking*, he thought. 'Anyway, how did you train the pigeons to mess up Penter's windows? I haven't seen any red circles above them.'

'I use different colours and shapes for different tasks,' said Durbrain proudly. 'Red circles for the playing fields. Green rectangles for Penter's windows.'

Sam pulled the aerial picture from his pocket and nodded at the red splodges marked there. 'And I guess you use these smaller pictures for one on one pigeon interaction, yeah?'

Durbrain grabbed it back. 'Wondered where I'd dropped that. Yeah, I do.'

Sam pointed to the main picture. 'So what does the green rectangle mean?'

'That ugly green roof on the Science Block!' chuckled Durbrain. 'Came in very handy. I taught the pigeons to associate pooing beneath a big green shape with a reward—gave them unpopped popcorn for every poop on target. They're quick learners.'

'That one who crashed into the window wasn't so quick,' Sam countered.

Durbrain shrugged. 'There are always a few stragglers in pigeon training.'

'Nevertheless, I have awarded that pigeon a medal for bravery,' Pacemaker announced, pulling what looked to be a foil-coated chocolate coin on a piece of ribbon from his pocket. 'The order of the bashed beak.'

To Sam it looked like one of the medals from Ashley's wounded soldier costume in the play. What was it doing here? 'Of course,' cried Sam. '*You* stole the boys' costumes!'

'Don't be impertinent, boy,' snapped Collier.

Suddenly there was a scrabbling sound at the main doors. Sam's hopes soared. Someone was coming to his rescue . . .

'Help!' he yelled.

Pacemaker's scrawny face turned scarlet. 'So you *don't* want to join us!'

'They've got me, help!' Sam cried again.

Durbrain opened the door and Daisy Pellock

burst in. She frowned at the sight of Sam. 'What are *you* doing here?'

'They're crazy!' he cried. 'Help me, quick, they're going to . . .'

'Ah, here you are, Daisy,' said Collier, calmly.

Sam's heart sank like a stone. 'So it's not just coincidence that so many of the costumes are red. You're in on this, too.'

'Got no choice,' she muttered.

'I take it back,' Sam told Pacemaker. 'Obviously you didn't steal the costumes. *She* did.'

Daisy shrugged. 'I didn't know which costume would make the best disguise for Mr Pacemaker. So I took the lot.'

Sam nodded. 'And so he became a monk to do over the Head's office.'

Pacemaker looked at him warningly. 'I'm no petty thief!'

Oh, I am sorry! You may be a kidnapper, an imposter, and a raving maniac but you're not a thief . . . 'Mr Penter told me some things were taken—'

'Oh, I took a *few* things, yes,' said Pacemaker, waving a hand airily. 'But only to make them *think* I was a thief. Daisy bundled up those

133

items with the costumes so they'd be found later.'

'Then why *did* you risk breaking in to the Head's office?'

The old man smiled slyly. 'I needed to know the layout of the enemy's lair. I needed to know where things were. For the *real* surprise we have in store for that short-sighted fool.'

'A hundred birds relieving themselves on our Head's head is just for starters,' whispered Collier. 'We will have a *big* surprise waiting for him after that.'

'Very big,' sniggered Durbrain.

'Very, *very*, big,' Pacemaker elaborated. 'Huge, in fact. Enormous!'

'I get the message,' Sam assured him.

'But in the meantime, gentlemen, we are presented with a bit of a poser, what?' Pacemaker advanced on him, his left eye twitching behind his monocle. 'What are we going to do with this boy, hmm? He knows too much!'

Sam frowned. 'Only because you've spent the last ten minutes telling me! That's not my fault, is it?' He paused. 'And I promise I won't tell anyone. Like, the police—who are going to be right on your tails, you know that, right?'

'No one will know we are involved,' declared Pacemaker. 'Not once you have tasted the dark juice of the mungleberry!'

Sam frowned. 'The what?'

'It's the natives' name for a rare type of berry we brought back from the jungles of Madagascar,' Collier explained, looking a little shifty.

'When pulped and mixed with certain other spices it affects the memory.' Pacemaker chuckled madly. 'Our meeting will seem no more real to you than a half-remembered dream!'

'A nightmare more like,' muttered Sam.

'With respect, Major, time is marching on,' Collier announced. 'We'll wait till everyone's on their way to the outdoor assembly and the coast is clear, then we'll lock Innocent away until this is all over.'

'Is the play still due to be performed at the start of this assembly, girl?' demanded Pacemaker.

Daisy nodded. 'That's what Mrs Flange said.'

'The Head is due to take to the stage when it's finished,' Killer mused. 'To congratulate the players dressed in their lovely, vivid red . . .'

'When the crowd applauds, the noise will carry all the way to here . . .' Pacemaker crowed.

'And *that's* my signal to release the pigeons,' said Durbrain triumphantly. 'Easy!'

'Mrs Flange and Fido have got everything prepared,' Daisy reported. 'The dress rehearsal's due to start in a minute.'

'That's a point,' said Sam. 'I'm needed for that—I'm playing the monk you impersonated this morning. Shame to spoil the play—why not let me go and do my bit? I promise I'll come back straight afterwards!'

Killer gave him a tired look. 'Is it a big part?'

'One little line,' said Durbrain.

'In that case, run along to the Drama Studio and tell them that Sam's been taken sick and has gone home. Tell them that *you* will appear in his place.'

'But I can't, sir!' Durbrain protested. 'You need me to send off the pigeons!'

'I'm well aware of that,' thundered Killer. 'You *tell* them you will perform—then don't turn up! Daisy will go to Mrs Flange with the monk's costume and announce you've had a bad case of stage fright and can't go on. It's only one line— they can find someone else, I'm sure.'

'But, sir, you can't do this!' Sam cried. 'You can't cheat the audience of my moving, sensitive portrayal of "Gloomy Monk". How could you ever live with yourself?'

'I think my years of dreary retirement will give me ample time to come to terms with my conscience,' said Killer darkly. 'Attend the rehearsal, Durban, then report back here to collect the Head's surprise from Major Pacemaker.' He checked his watch and sighed. 'Now I suppose *I* must attend this dratted lunch . . .'

In desperation, Sam tried to make a break for it through the door as Collier opened it. But Pacemaker grabbed him by the collar and yanked him back.

'Don't hurt him!' said Daisy, worriedly.

'I'm with you on that one,' gasped Sam.

'Don't be so soft, girl,' snapped Pacemaker, pushing Sam into a chair. 'No harm in a bit of rough and tumble! Made me the man I am today.'

'Yeah, a king-sized fruit loop,' muttered Sam. He looked up at Daisy and saw how worried she looked. Scared even. Out of her depth. And he knew just how she felt.

Gloomy Monk had hit the nail right on the head, Sam decided: '*Oooh, what a calamity.*'

In the Drama Studio, Sara stepped forward on the marked-out stage to deliver the final speech in a word-perfect performance: 'And so, after many centuries—' it certainly felt like many centuries to Sara—'we come to today at Freekham High. The last day in Mr Collier's long career. This school has been like a second home for him . . . not always a happy home, perhaps, since it's stuffed full of strangers and smart-alecs he has to shout at every day. But at least there are no beds to make . . .'

She shot a look at Fido—he had promised her he would take all the blame if the Head told her off for being cheeky, but she told him she wasn't bothered. Since this was her last day, it hardly mattered much what the Head thought of her. What *did* matter was . . . what had happened to Sam? Taken suddenly ill, according to Durbrain—but what would *he* know about it? Sara wasn't sure she could believe a word he said. Maybe Sam was suffering stage fright, and the Gloomy Monk was doing a gloomy bunk? No, more likely he was up to something. Some crazy stunt or other . . .

But why get Durbrain involved with it? Sam hardly knew him . . .

Memphis, prompting in the wings, took Sara's daydreaming for temporary amnesia: 'We wish him a long and happy retirement . . .' she hissed.

'We wish him a long and happy retirement,' said Sara quickly, smiling out at her imaginary audience. 'And to you, dear audience, we wish a lazy, carefree summer holiday. May the sun for ever shine high . . . on Freekham High.'

Fido and Flange clapped enthusiastically. 'Lovely!' cried Fido.

'Well done, everyone,' said Flange. 'Good work, Dennis. You made a very good short-notice stand-in monk.'

'Just don't make a habit of it,' Fido added, to a few groans and half-hearted titters.

'All right, everybody,' Flange went on. 'Take your costumes with you—don't lose them—and enjoy what's left of lunchtime. We'll meet again by the stage on the playing fields when the bell goes for outdoor assembly.'

Durbrain headed hastily to the door. Sara started after him: 'Hey, Dennis, I need to talk to you. You said you used a tape recorder to make the ghostly sounds—'

'Did I?' He looked blank. 'Oh yeah, I did. Yeah.'

She grabbed hold of his sleeve as he made to leave. 'Well, I played the tape in the storeroom and there were no ghosts on it.'

'What tape?' His heavy brow folded into deep creases. 'Oh . . . uh . . . I used a different one. But I've chucked it away now.'

Sara looked at him dubiously. 'You know what? Whatever. But tell me properly, where is Sam? You said he was—'

'Gotta run,' said Durbrain shiftily. He pulled free and fled from the room.

'Everything OK?' asked Memphis.

'I guess,' said Sara. 'It's just weird that Sam would go off sick and only tell Durbrain. What was he even *doing* with Durbrain?'

'Dunno. He was giving him a good grilling about pigeons in Gricey's lesson . . .' Memphis shrugged. 'I saw Sam in the canteen at the start of lunchtime and he looked fine. He said he'd see me at dress rehearsal.'

'There's been something not quite right about him all day,' said Sara gloomily.

Memphis looked slightly sheepish. 'You wanna know what's up? I found out.'

'What?'

'It's Sam's last day too.'

'*What?*' Sara's stomach twisted. 'No way!' She stared at Memphis. 'He's *moving*?'

'Uh-huh. Another one of those freaky Freekham coincidences that always happen to you two.'

'Guess so.' But deep down, it seemed to Sara that it was more than just chance. It was as if the *school*—new on the surface but old underneath—had drawn them together into a life that was weird and freaky and strange . . . but fun. Now they were both walking out on it. Sam, apparently, had already gone.

Their time had run out and she hadn't even known it.

'Do you think he's just *gone*, then?' Sara whispered. 'Disappeared out of my life without even saying goodbye?'

'Sara Knot, you are *so* into him!'

'It's not that!' Sara protested. 'It's just . . . well, why didn't he tell me he was going?'

'Why didn't *you* tell *him*?'

She paused, looked at Memphis suspiciously. 'He doesn't know this is my last day, does he?'

'How *could* he know?' said Memphis with a strange, tinkly laugh. 'Oh, Sara, I just can't believe you're *both* going. It could be like the ravens leaving the Tower of London,' she joked. 'Bad times ahead for Freekham High.'

'You don't think something's happened to Sam . . . ?'

'He'll be fine,' Memphis assured her. 'Probably just bunking. Hiding out somewhere.'

Sara shook her head. Something didn't feel quite right. The noises in the storeroom, the dizzy light-headedness she'd felt, the thief who took the costumes and gave back all he'd stolen, Daisy looking so worried over something secret . . . There were mysteries here as yet unsolved. And Sam had never walked out on a mystery yet . . .

She jumped suddenly. It was as if someone had tugged on a loose thread in her head.

'You OK?' asked Memphis.

'Hiding out, you said.' Sara grabbed hold of Memphis's elbows. 'Why was Durbrain hiding there *then*?'

'You've lost me.'

'Why did Durbrain go and hide in the store-room at Breather and play the ghost? No one was around to hear him, so what made him rush all the way over to a stinky old storeroom on the off-chance someone would walk by—especially when he had to get off to the computer lab straight after?'

Memphis raised her eyebrows. 'They don't call him Durbrain for nothing.'

'And all week he's been saying there's no such thing as that ghost. If it was him all the time, tricking everyone, then why wasn't he trying to build it up more?' Sara thought hard. 'Memph! What if he overheard me and Fido telling Flange we were going to that storeroom?'

'But if he had, he wouldn't have gone there, would he? Even *he* wouldn't be that stupid. He would know that you were bound to find him there and catch him at it.'

'Unless he *wanted* to get caught!'

'Sara, you are seriously crushing my elbows.' Memphis gently extricated herself. 'Kick back a sec. Why would Durbrain *want* to get caught?'

'So suddenly everyone thinks that *he's* the ghost!' Sara looked at Memphis. 'Any other noises people hear, they'll put down to one of his tapes or that dodgy boiler he reckons he knows all about. But I heard the ghost again in that storeroom after Durbrain confessed. And no way were those noises on tape.'

Memphis frowned. 'Are you sure?'

'I am now. At the time I felt kind of weird, but . . .' She nodded. 'There was this big lunch box in there, too. Freshly packed. Durbrain tripped over it but I don't think it was his . . .'

'Was it made of metal?' Memphis asked quickly. 'Sort of pale blue, scratched, and old?'

Sara blinked. 'How did you know?'

'Daisy Pellock was carrying a box like that, down by the farm. Me and Sam saw her.' She scratched her head. 'But why would she have dumped it in that storeroom?'

'I don't know. But she was really upset earlier. Said she was involved in something bad . . .' Sara chewed her lip. 'Memph, there's no such thing as ghosts, right?'

'I guess.'

'And yet someone's been making those noises,

haven't they? Someone real, who needs to eat . . . Someone locked up! Daisy brings him food in secret. And when all his groans and cries and banging noises attract too much attention, Durbrain pretends it was him all the time so no one gets suspicious!'

'Sara, that is a mad theory,' Memphis laughed, 'even by Sam's standards. You would have *seen* someone locked in the storeroom!'

'Maybe not . . . The storeroom doesn't go as deep as it's meant to—Penter pointed it out.'

'*Penter?* What does Penter have to do with—?'

'Never mind that now,' said Sara quickly. 'The Humanities Block was built up around the old science block, remember? Maybe there's a part of it hidden behind the storeroom wall— behind the filing cabinet maybe—and *that's* where this person is being held! Maybe he's knocked over some old chemicals, and that's what the stink is! I'll bet that's what made me feel so light-headed, too!'

'Come off it,' said Memphis. 'If that was true, about the only person old enough to know that place existed would be—'

'Killer Collier.' Sara nodded. 'Who's being forced to retire and who is not very happy about it. Who's just overturned Durbrain the Freekham ghost's crummy grade and given him an A minus for no apparent reason.'

Memphis wasn't laughing now. 'And Durbrain was the last person to see Sam—who's suddenly gone missing, just like that.' She bit her lip. 'Jeez, Sara. If you're right about this . . . What are we going to do? Check out the storeroom?'

'I think we should call in the big guns straight away,' said Sara. 'Why don't you try to find Daisy or Durbrain, and see if you can get some proper answers? I'll go find the Head and tell him what we know.'

'He'll probably laugh in your face.'

'If I'm wrong and I'm making a total fool of myself, who cares? I'm out of here in an hour or so and never coming back.' She frowned. 'But if I'm right . . .'

They looked at each other for a few moments. Then Sara spun on her heel and ran from the Drama Studio.

* * *

Sam sat in the Farm Block classroom with Daisy, wondering what on earth he was going to do. The long minutes crawled by in silence. The dress rehearsal must be over by now.

'So how come you got involved with this bunch of loonies?' he asked. 'I mean, I can see why someone like Durbrain might, but . . .'

Daisy was looking at the floor. 'Collier wanted someone involved with a bit more common sense than Durbrain.'

'Common sense. Right.' He shook his head. 'They are totally crazy!'

'I'm helping them for my dad's sake,' said Daisy fiercely. 'All I've really done is put lots of red in the costumes and look after Mr Ferret for them, making sure he's OK, giving him food and stuff.' She frowned. 'Except I didn't have time to hand over his food at Breather. Durbrain tipped me off that Fido and Sara were coming, I had to ditch and pitch . . .'

Sam stared at her. 'Where *is* Ferret?'

'Locked up behind the storeroom in the Humanities Block.' She sighed. 'Where *you're* going to end up.'

'Will you listen to yourself? "*Locked up*"? That's against the law!'

'He's only been kept there for three days,' she argued weakly. 'Collier was sneaking Pacemaker and Durbrain in at weekends and after school—but then Ferret found there were too many pigeons in his loft and got suspicious. He had to be put out of the way—somewhere we could look after him easily.'

'Look after?! We're talking kidnapping here!' Sam told her angrily.

Daisy shook her head. 'He won't remember anything about it. The mungleberry juice—'

'You really believe that rubbish?' Sam shook his head. 'Pacemaker's mad as a stoat. How can berries wipe your memory? Unless a crate of them falls on your head, maybe.'

'Just you wait.' Daisy looked pale and tired. 'Ferret drinks the juice each day and hardly knows where he is.'

'So what're you going to do—leave a lifetime's supply in our kitchens when you let us go?' Sam gave her a scornful look. 'Anyway, don't forget—he's just a *teacher*! I'm made of tougher stuff, and *I* won't forget all this, whatever happens!

I'll go to the cops and *you* will get arrested for helping them do this. So how is that going to help your dad exactly?'

'I don't care what happens to me,' said Daisy bravely. 'But when Collier and Pacemaker do what they're going to do, my dad will get the benefit.'

'He's a builder, isn't he?' said Sam, frowning. 'What do you mean, "benefit"?'

'You'll find out soon enough,' she sighed. 'Everyone will.'

There was a clatter from outside. Through the glass in the door, Sam saw Durbrain enter and dump the monk outfit on the floor. Then Pacemaker emerged and handed him a large cardboard box.

'You're sure you know where to place this, boy?' said the major.

Durbrain nodded. 'Inside the low cupboard opposite his desk. Then I set the trip wire so the cupboard door opens when the next person comes in.'

'Off you go then.'

'Tripwire?' Sam looked at Daisy. 'Just what are they planning to do to the Head?'

'Don't worry, he'll have plenty of time to get clear,' she said firmly.

Sam felt sick. 'Clear of what?'

'He's just going to get a fright, that's all. A big joke, Collier says. A very big joke.' She looked down. 'But the important thing is that my dad will get a good rebuilding contract out of it.'

'Rebuilding?' Sam jumped up. 'Daisy, *tell me what's in that box*!'

But Daisy had started crying, and it seemed she couldn't stop.

The Head wasn't in his office, so Sara went to the debating rooms to see if Collier's special celebration lunch was going to end any time soon.

But it was still in full swing.

You could hear the raucous merriment from the next block. The teachers were in total party mode, laughing, shouting . . . Sara remembered how giggly she'd gone when she was here before, how even Penter had been affected.

'Chemicals,' she told herself. '*Freaky* chemicals.'

Sara had hoped she would be able to collar the Head, but she soon realized she didn't stand a chance. It was carnage in there—complete tutor meltdown! Penter and Madame Rille the French teacher were tunelessly singing some ancient crumbly love song in a duet, while Miss Bedfellow danced on one of the tables, leering round at her fellow teachers. The Maths master, Mr McLennon, was laughing at nothing at all, his face bright red, his wispy hair standing up all over the place. Softy Steen the social studies teacher was trying to do disco moves to impress the Head's secretary, whirling his tweed jacket around his head.

Sara cringed. It was the most embarrassing thing she had ever seen. And worst of all, Collier was sitting close beside the Head. Even he was chortling away while the Head rocked in his chair, back and forth, back and forth—until eventually the chair toppled over backwards and the Head fell heavily on to the floor, laughing like a drain.

She decided she would wait for the Head in his office, when hopefully Collier would not be there. He was bound to call in at his office before going out to see the play. She wondered if she should have some strong coffee waiting for him.

If he was ever going to take her seriously he'd need to sober up fast.

It was nearly time for afternoon registration by the time she reached the Head's office. Just as she approached, she saw the door open just a little—and Durbrain come sneaking out from inside.

'You!' she hissed. 'I want a word with you. What were you doing in there?'

He froze like a rabbit caught in the headlights of an articulated lorry. 'None of your business!'

'I think it might be the Head's business.' She folded her arms. 'Where's Sam? And I want the truth.'

'He's better off out of it,' said Durbrain, starting to run off. 'And so will you be. Just don't go into the Head's office, all right? Don't stick your nose in—or you'll regret it!'

'You're in big trouble, Durbrain!' Sara yelled after him. 'Just you wait!'

Don't go into the Head's office indeed. Clearly he had been up to no good. She'd better see what he had done.

Sara pushed open the door and peered inside. Nothing seemed disturbed. She entered the office.

Too late, she noticed the tripwire.

As her leg caught against it and pulled it taut, a cupboard door swung open. Something big, black, and round tumbled out and hit the floor with a metallic clang. Sara gasped as the object bounced and rolled across the floor towards her, coming to rest against the tip of her shoe.

It looked like a big bomb. And just in case anyone was in any doubt, the word BOMB had been daubed over it in huge white letters. It looked ridiculous and menacing all at once, like the bombs you got in old cartoons.

But it was ticking.

Sara stared down at it, so horrified she could barely breathe. *Durbrain, I'm going to kill you!*

The floor wasn't even, had a slight slope to it. If she moved her foot the ticking device would roll away—maybe go off!

But if she stayed . . . How long before it went off anyway?

'Help!' she shouted. 'Anyone there? Help!'

No answer. She thought of the teachers, dancing and laughing and joking. The Head flat out on the floor, his assistant transfixed by Softy

Steen's disco moves. They wouldn't be coming back in a hurry.

She couldn't even reach the phone on the desk.

This was crazy! It couldn't be a bomb. Of course it couldn't. It was just a joke! Just . . .

Just in case it wasn't, Sara stood stock-still. She was frozen with fear.

Tick. Tick. Tick, went the bomb. *Tick. Tick. Tick.*

Afternoon Registration

Tick. Tick. Tick. Tick. Tick. Tick. Tick. Tick. Tick.
Tick. Tick. Tick. Tick. Tick. Tick. Tick. Tick. Tick.
Tick. Tick. Tick. Tick. Tick. Tick. Tick. Tick. Tick.
Tick. Tick. Tick. Tick. Tick. Tick. Tick. Tick. Tick.
Tick. Tick. Tick. Tick. Tick. Tick. Tick. Tick. Tick.
Tick. Tick. Tick. Tick. Tick. Tick. Tick. Tick. Tick.
Tick. Tick. Tick. Tick. Tick. Tick. Tick. Tick. Tick.
Tick. Tick. Tick. Tick. Tick. Tick. Tick. Tick. Tick.
Tick. Tick. Tick. Tick. Tick. Tick. Tick. Tick. Tick.
Tick. Tick. Tick. Tick. Tick. Tick. Tick. Tick. Tick.
Tick. Tick. Tick. Tick. Tick. Tick. Tick. Tick. Tick.
Tick. Tick. Tick. Tick. Tick. Tick. Tick. Tick. Tick.
Tick. Tick. Tick. Tick. Tick. Tick. Tick. Tick. Tick.
Tick. Tick. Tick. Tick. Tick. Tick. Tick. Tick. Tick.
Tick. Tick. Tick. Tick. Tick. Tick. Tick. Tick. Tick.
Tick. Tick. Tick. Tick. Tick. Tick. Tick. Tick. Tick.
Tick. Tick. Tick. Tick. Tick. Tick. Tick. Tick. Tick.
Tick. Tick. Tick. Tick. Tick. Tick. Tick. Tick. Tick.

Tick. Tick. Tick. Tick. Tick. Tick. Tick. Tick. Tick.
Tick. Tick. Tick. Tick. Tick. Tick. Tick. Tick. Tick.
Tick. Tick. Tick. Tick. Tick. Tick. Tick. Tick. Tick.
Tick. Tick. Tick. Tick. Tick. Tick. Tick. Tick. Tick.
Tick. Tick. Tick. Tick. Tick. Tick. Tick. Tick. Tick.
Tick. Tick. Tick. Tick. Tick. Tick. Tick. Tick. Tick.
Tick. Tick. Tick. Tick. Tick. Tick. Tick. Tick. Tick.
Tick. Tick. Tick. Tick. Tick. Tick. Tick . . .

PERIODS SEVEN AND EIGHT
END OF TERM ASSEMBLY

As the hooter sounded the end of afternoon registration, the words Sam had been dreading were uttered. 'Time to take our little spy away,' said Major Pacemaker, poking his head into the classroom.

Daisy looked at him through teary eyes. 'Aren't you worried about being seen?'

'It's too late to stop us now,' said Pacemaker with a jubilant smile. 'Besides, most people will be on their way to the playing fields. And if anyone asks, I am a frail old friend of Mr Collier's, here to see him off on his final day, and the boy here is helping me to get about.' He chuckled. 'I shall be leaning on him quite heavily, to make sure he doesn't shout or try to run away.'

'What has Durbrain put in the Head's office?' Sam demanded.

'I'm not wasting any more breath on you, boy!' said Pacemaker.

They headed off, the three of them. Daisy looked forlorn, clutching the red monk's habit. Pacemaker staggered along behind Sam, using him like a human Zimmer frame, bony hands clamped around his arms to stop him dashing away. Sam thought about shouting for help, but there was no one to hear him, no one at all, all the way to the Humanities Block.

Until suddenly, Softy Steen burst out through the main doors.

'Sir!' cried Sam. 'Help, I'm being kidnapped!'

Steen stared at him, red-faced and puffy eyed. Then he looked at Pacemaker and frowned.

And then he burst out laughing. 'Oh, Sam! That's a good one!'

'It's true! And there's this plot to get a load of pigeons to poo on the headmaster and—'

Steen laughed even harder. 'Oh, Sam, mate, you're priceless.' He staggered off. 'Sorry, got to scoot. I think I'm late taking my class to the play . . .'

'Sir, *please*!' Sam begged. But Steen was

laughing so loudly he couldn't hear. What the hell was wrong with him?

'Try that once more, boy,' murmured Pacemaker, 'and you're in real trouble.'

Sam snorted as he was shoved through the main doors. 'Like it could get worse.'

But something told him that from the look on Daisy's face, it could.

Sara felt a trickle of sweat dart down the back of her neck. She was still holding herself absolutely motionless. The bomb—no, scratch that, the *thing*, that sounded less scary— was still ticking. And she was still calling for help—but there was no one around. Distantly she could hear the sound of shoes scuffing on concrete and deranged laughter from a teacher or two as people made their way to the playing fields. At least if the *thing* went off there would be no one else inside to be hurt . . .

She stared down at it. 'If you turn out to be just a metal bowling ball, I'm going to look really, really stupid.'

It just sat there. *Tick. Tick. Tick.*

Sara crossed all her fingers. '*Please* turn out to be just a metal bowling ball!'

Tick. Tick. Tick.

Risk it, she thought. *Run!*

Yeah, right.

When I don't turn up for the play, people will come looking, she decided. *They'll find me. And if they* don't, *well, it's the Head's office. He'll call in, in a minute. Looks like a speech on his desk, must be for assembly . . .*

She winced. Judging by the state of the Head in the debating chamber, he'd probably barge inside, grab the bomb and try to juggle it with a couple of oranges.

I'm doomed, thought Sara. *It's bye-bye Freekham High, all right . . .*

Tick. Tick. Tick.

Sam was being marched inexorably closer to the storeroom in the Humanities Block.

'Someone's coming,' Daisy said nervously, hearing footsteps up ahead.

'We'll hide behind the staircase!' Pacemaker

announced. He shoved Sam out of sight and clamped a hand over his mouth.

Sam's eyes widened to see the Head and Collier staggering along the corridor together, clinging to each other as if they were scared to let go. Clearly they were on the same stuff as Steen.

'Well, that was a jolly good send-off,' giggled Collier. 'Thank you, dear boy.'

'It is I who should thank *you*, Lionel,' the Head retorted. 'What a hoot! I haven't laughed so much in years.'

'Having met your wife, I can quite understand,' said Killer. Then the two of them burst out into hysterical laughter.

Sam's spirits were already low, but now they were sinking through the soles of his feet and pooling on the polished floor. Even if he *could* get away, the Head was in no fit state to heed any kind of warning.

'I must just pop back to my office,' the Head said weakly between titters. 'I need to pick up the notes for my post-play speech.'

'Oh, never mind that,' Killer said quickly. 'Let's go straight to the playing fields. Don't worry

161

about your speech. You can say the play has left you . . . speechless!'

Again they laughed like drains.

'And I think I can assure you,' said Killer, 'you will certainly be *struck* by the *raw strength* of *one particular performance* . . . Though I've never cared much for theatre myself. Strictly . . . *for the birds*!'

Sam winced. There were enough ominous hints in that little speech to stuff a pigeon loft, but the Head just tottered off drunkenly, arm in arm with Collier. Silly old fool. Serve him right, whatever had been put in his office . . .

But Sam wasn't about to let this pair of geriatric pigeon-crazed maniacs get the better of him and ruin the play. Not Sara's starring role, after all the work she had put into it. He just had to bide his time and hope that a chance presented itself.

Once all was quiet again, Pacemaker shuffled them out of hiding and they continued on their way. The tang of chemicals hung in the air around the storeroom, as if a radioactive skunk had been busy nearby. Daisy went to unlock the door—but it was already open.

'That's weird,' she said. And then she giggled.

'I fail to see what is funny,' said Pacemaker. 'The sooner you're locked away, lad, the better.' And then he giggled too.

'You two are mental,' said Sam darkly. No way was he about to giggle. Instead, he let out a belly laugh.

'Are we going in then, or what?' said Daisy.

'I vote "what",' Sam told her. '*What* is a much better idea.'

Pacemaker chuckled. 'Stop messing about, boy,' he said, and pushed Sam inside. 'Oh, I must say I feel quite peculiar.'

'Sort of light-headed?' Sam wondered.

'Me too!' said Daisy.

'Must be some sort of laughing gas!' cried Pacemaker.

The idea of laughing gas seemed hilarious, and soon all three were whooping with laughter.

Until someone else joined in, chuckling in the shadows.

'Who's that?' gasped Pacemaker.

'The Freekham ghost!' spluttered Sam, his ribs aching with mirth.

Pacemaker yelped as, from out of the gloom,

a mop bopped him on the head. With a big, silly grin on his face, he sank to the floor.

Sam and Daisy stared down at him in shock. Then Sam looked up to find Memphis standing there, leaning on the mop for support.

And all three of them burst out in hysterics.

'Sara reckoned someone was shut up in here,' Memphis explained, between giggles. 'She went to find the Head . . . and when she and Penter never showed for afternoon reg I thought maybe they were down here checking it out . . . so then I thought maybe *I'd* better check it out before the play started and . . .' She nodded to Pacemaker. 'And then I heard this creep say something about locking you up, Sam—'

'I owe you big time, Memphis,' said Sam, taking the mop off her. 'You *wiped the floor* with him!'

Again, they burst out guffawing. But then Daisy burst into tears. 'It's all over, isn't it?' she wailed.

'Correct,' said Sam, waving the mop at her. 'So just let him out.'

'Who?' asked Memphis.

'The Ferret in the mousehole,' Sam told her.

Daisy wrestled away the filing cabinet to reveal a makeshift door in the wall, made of thick wood. A muffled cry came from inside. The door was secured to the wall with bolts top and bottom, so Daisy undid them, giggling one moment, sobbing the next. She swung open the door to reveal an eerie glow. The cries were suddenly a lot less muffled, more urgent, and they echoed strangely.

'You two get outside,' Sam suggested, 'go to a window and get some fresh air! And watch her, Memphis.'

'I will—as soon as my double-vision wears off,' she said woozily.

'Here.' Daisy held out a small key to Sam. 'You'll need this.'

He tittered. 'But the door is open!'

'It's not for the door.'

Sam ducked inside through the low opening, and found himself in a small, windowless room lit with a flickering oil lamp. It stank of must and sulphur and chemicals. Two rusty vents were placed high in the mouldering walls—which could explain why the smell was carrying into the neighbouring classrooms. Old, damp boxes were stacked high, together with dusty bottles half filled with evil-looking liquids, and there was a gaping hole in the wet, sticky floor. Risking a quick peer inside, Sam saw a big black pipeline which had also been cracked open. Broken glass crunched under his feet as he crossed over to the large, wriggling figure slumped in one corner.

'Mr Ferret!' Sam gasped, his head clearing a little. No longer did everything seem quite so hilarious. He pulled down the gag tied around the teacher's mouth.

'I know you, don't I?' said Mr Ferret. He didn't smell too good, and Sam didn't even want to think what might lurk within the metal bucket beside him, but otherwise he seemed fine—except his hands were handcuffed and his ankle weighed down by a rusty ball and chain. Aha, that was why Daisy gave him the key.

'It's me, Sam Innocent, sir,' he said, going to work on the locks. 'You've been kidnapped!'

'I have?' He smiled suddenly as his hands were freed. 'Then I don't *live* here? Thank goodness!'

Sam moved on to the ball and chain. 'Don't you remember what happened?'

'Everything's a bit of a blur . . . I keep getting these funny dreams.'

'And you groan in your sleep, I'll bet,' muttered Sam, thinking of the ghostly moans that had carried from here through the vents.

Ferret smiled brightly as Sam removed the chain. 'Still, the food's been good! This nice girl pops in with it from time to time!'

Sam couldn't believe that the big bear of a man had been kept here in this little place for days. How could he be so calm about this—was it all down to the freaky laughing gas? Then he spotted a flask on the floor and took a cautious sniff. It smelt sour but fruity.

Mungleberry? So perhaps it *did* work . . .

Sam shuddered and threw it over his shoulder, where it smashed against one of the glass jars.

'Don't!' said Ferret. 'This place is falling apart as it is! Look at that hole in the floor . . .' He tutted. 'This big cylinder of gas or something fell off the top shelf and smashed right through the floor. Then it started hissing—leaking!—so I had to hide it out of the way. In the big pipe.'

Sam glanced back at the hole in the floor.

This place was an old chemical store—obviously this was the source of the laughing gas. It must have leaked out from here into the surrounding area . . .

'I've been putting lots of rubbish into that pipe to get it out of the way,' Ferret went on with a giggle. 'Not really anywhere else to put it. And not very easy when you're cuffed and chained, I can tell you!'

'Yeah, I think some people heard you "tidying",' said Sam, thinking back to the clanking noises in Biology. If these underground pipes joined the whole school together then the noise was bound to carry . . . 'Come on, sir. Time to go, I reckon.'

'Why do you call me sir?' He beamed as he stood up, taking the oil lamp from its perch on a box to light their way. 'Am I a knight, then?'

'No.' Sam patted his hand comfortingly. 'I'm afraid you're . . . a teacher.'

'*What?*' A frown appeared on Ferret's big features. 'Are—are you sure?'

'I'm sorry to be the one to tell you.'

'Oh my *God*!' Ferret looked appalled. 'Me? A *teacher*?' After all that he had been through, this news was clearly enough to push the big man over the edge. He slumped heavily back against a pile of boxes, sending a couple crashing to the floor with a sound of breaking glass. Liquid leaked out from within, pooling on the floor.

'Quick,' said Sam, offering the heartbroken Ferret his hand. 'Let's get out of here. And you can leave the lamp. You won't be needing it any more.'

Sam led him carefully out through the hole in the wall. When Ferret noticed Pacemaker on the floor of the dingy storeroom, his frown deepened.

'Wait a minute,' he said. 'I remember that man. He and Mr . . . Mr Collier . . . *Another* teacher.' The frown became a scowl. 'They trussed me up like a turkey and put me in here! And they . . . they were doing something with my pigeons!' Suddenly he started to snigger.

'Don't get too happy now,' said Sam, dragging him out of the storeroom. 'We've got a lot to sort out . . .'

'Sam!' Memphis ran over from the classroom opposite. No laughter now, she looked dead serious. 'Daisy's told me what Collier's been planning.'

'I know all about the pigeons—'

'But did you know about the bomb?'

If Sam's jaw had dropped any lower it would have bruised his toes. He stared at Daisy, who was slumped in a chair by the open window, her head in her hands. 'Is *that* what was in the box Durbrain took to the Head?'

'Only a small one,' she said feebly. 'And no one will get hurt—they promised! It's got a timer on it, see, so there'll be ages to get everybody out. They just want to blow up his office—'

'So they can swing your dad the rebuilding work!' Sam cried. 'And you actually *believed* them? These people are crazy!'

'I had to help my dad somehow!' Daisy wailed.

'By blowing up half the school?' Sam crossed to the window and took a few deep lungfuls of fresh air. He needed it.

Memphis put a hand on his shoulder. 'Sam, Sara went off to find the Head to tell him about the storeroom. Neither of them are here.'

'She'll be on stage doing the play by now, won't she?' asked Sam.

Memphis checked her watch. 'It should have started—'

'Where's Sara? Where is she?' yelled Fido, bursting into the classroom, making them all jump. 'Memphis! What the hell are you doing, prompter? And Sam! Durbrain said you'd gone home, and now *he's* vanished . . .' He pointed to the red habit in Daisy's lap. 'Daisy, what are you doing with Sam's costume? I mean, *Durbrain's* costume. I mean . . .' He snatched it off her, staring round wildly. 'I've been looking everywhere for Sara. The last teacher's finally arrived with his class, we're ready to start the play, and there's no sign of her!'

'Did you check the Head's office?' asked Memphis.

'No. Why would I?'

Memphis looked at Sam gravely.

'I'm on it,' he told her, sprinting to the door. 'Memphis, Daisy—get Ferret and Pacemaker outside. Then call the police. And hit the fire alarms, Memph, we have to make sure the school is empty.'

'What? Who? Where?' Fido threw his arms up in the air. 'What about my play? Without a narrator, it's going to bomb!'

'You don't know the half of it,' Sam assured

him. 'I'll explain everything later. For now, just get out of here, back to the stage.'

'But what am I going to—'

'Do the narrating yourself, you div!' shouted Sam. 'The show must go on—we can't have anyone coming back near the school.'

Fido held up the habit. 'What about the missing monk?'

Sam snatched away the costume and chucked it in the bin. 'Trust me, there's enough red on that stage already.'

'You've flipped!' said Fido.

'Very probably,' Sam agreed. 'Now *go*!'

Fido, utterly bewildered, ran back out.

'What are you going to do, Sam?' Memphis said. 'Are you really cut out to play the action hero? All you've ever played was the fool and truant!'

'Don't forget, I almost played a Gloomy Monk,' Sam said, turning to go. 'So I'll say my prayers and see you soon.' He sprinted off along the corridor towards the Head's office and muttered under his breath: 'I hope.'

Sara heard the fire alarm going off, and that

made up her mind. She wasn't about to get roasted as well as blown to bits. She would make a move. She would definitely creep slowly away.

Tick. Tick.

Or make a dash for it.

Tick. Tick. Tick.

But if she crept too slowly, the thing might go off.

And if she ran she might jog the thing, and it might *still* go off.

She needed to clear her mind and think. But that was easier said than done when a *thing* was ticking against your toes and the doorbell from hell was ringing outside.

Suddenly there was a knock at the door. 'Hello?'

'Sam!' Sara cried. 'Get out of here!'

He opened the door and his head peered round. 'Well, that's charming, since I just ran all this way to see if you were all right.'

'One thing I am not is "all right"!' said Sara gravely. She pointed down to the thing at her feet. 'Look!'

'That's never a bomb!' said Sam sniffily.

She wasn't sure whether to be relieved or insulted by the strength of his conviction. 'It's ticking!' she told him.

'That's, like, a comedy bomb!' Sam complained. 'Are you sure?'

'Course I'm sure. It's like something out of a rubbishy panto! Look how old-fashioned it is . . .' He trailed off, and Sara's hopes dwindled. 'Ah, yes. Look how old-fashioned its *owners* are.'

'Collier?'

'And Major Pacemaker.' He stepped cautiously into the room. 'Long story—here are the edited highlights: pigeons, training, the colour red, Durbrain, old soldiers, Daisy, droppings, headmaster—revenge.'

'I figured it was something like that,' said Sara coolly. 'Now, Sam, *please*, call the police! Call the army! Call my mum! I can't stand here like this much longer.'

'Memphis is getting help. How long since you tripped the wire?'

'Twenty-one minutes and forty-six seconds. Roughly.'

'Then there may not be enough time to wait

for the coppers to get here.' Gently, Sam dropped down on one knee at her feet.

'What are you doing?' she hissed. 'This is not the best time to tell me you want to marry me!'

'Get over yourself,' he told her sharply. Then his voice softened. 'Funny, though. Whatever happens right now . . . things will never be the same, will they?'

Sara shook her head. 'I hear you're leaving Freekham,' she said simply.

He looked up. 'I hear *you* are, too.'

'Memphis has a big mouth,' they decided together.

Sara sighed miserably. 'I wanted to go out in style, not up in smoke.'

Sam looked back down. 'It's an ugly big thing, isn't it?'

'You should try having it ticking against your foot.'

'I was *talking* about your foot.'

Sara bunched her fists. 'Can you never be serious? You are a really nice guy, Sam, but sometimes you drive me crazy!'

'It's this place that's crazy,' Sam murmured. 'Freekham High.' He puffed out a big breath.

'Even so, after all the freaky stuff that's happened to us here, I never thought that this would be the way things ended . . .'

'It's not fair,' sighed Sara.

'Kind of fits, though, I guess,' said Sam, slowly lowering his head to the *thing*. 'We started off the madness here. Now we're finishing it.'

'And *it* is finishing *us* at the same time!' said Sara.

'You could always tell me to run off and save myself,' Sam suggested.

Sara smiled weakly. 'What, when we're having something like a meaningful conversation for once?'

'You're such a girl.'

'Thanks for noticing.'

Sam sniffed the *thing* cautiously. 'Can't smell gunpowder or anything.'

'Do you know what it smells like?'

'I know what your *foot* smells like, now—and believe me, that's too much information.'

'Will you leave my feet alone?'

'I only wish I—' Suddenly Sam went rigid. 'I can hear whirring! Something's happening inside!' He grabbed the *thing* in both hands and snatched it away from her foot. 'Run, Sara!'

'I—I can't just leave you!' she shouted. 'Get rid of that thing!'

'Where?'

'The window!'

Sam chucked it. It smacked into the glass, dropped on to the windowsill, and bounced back on to the floor.

'You could have opened the window first!' Sara wailed.

'You never said anything about opening the window first!' Sam wailed back.

Now the *thing* was rolling back towards them. Sara and Sam grabbed hold of each other.

'Bye,' said Sara.

'Bye,' said Sam.

And the thing knocked against the leg of the Head's desk.

Sara shut her eyes and clutched Sam tight.

BRRR-RRRRRRRR-INNNNG!

Something was ringing. A higher pitch than the fire alarm.

She opened her eyes and saw the *thing* had cracked open like an egg.

And inside it was an alarm clock.

Just an alarm clock.

Sam cleared his throat. His eyes were probably open too. But she was holding him so close that all he could see was a really good view of her ear.

They sprang apart, flustered. Sara kept staring at the ringing *thing*. Finally, it shut up, and went on ticking to itself. *Tick. Tick. Tick.*

They looked at each other. Then they cheered and whooped and burst into hysterical laughter, dancing around the Head's office for joy.

Then Sam seemed to recover himself. 'I *told* you it wasn't a real bomb,' he said loftily.

'You didn't know for sure!' Sara protested.

'I did!' he argued. 'Do you seriously think I would have stayed with you if I didn't know for sure it was a fake?'

Sara looked at him. 'Yes.' She half-smiled. 'Actually, I do seriously think that.'

'You're crazy,' he said. But before he turned his back she caught the blushes he was trying to hide.

'So all this was just a big sick joke,' Sara realized.

'Daisy said Collier described it as a big joke,'

said Sam, picking up the pieces of the so-called bomb. 'But she thought it was for real.'

Sara pulled a face. 'I'm not sure the police are going to be too impressed with us.'

'Oh, I think they'll be glad they came when they meet Major Pacemaker. You know, he and Collier kidnapped Ferret! *He's* the Freekham ghost!'

Sara gasped. 'No way! Is he OK?'

'Yeah, he's all right. Well, you know, all right for a *teacher*.'

She shot him a look. 'Who is this Pacemaker guy, anyway?'

'I'll tell you all about it,' said Sam. 'Now we're out of danger, we can—' He broke off. '*We* may be out of danger . . . but the Head's not! I sent Fido off to take your part in the play—'

'Fido?! He'll look lousy in my red cape!'

'—and when it's finished, and the crowd go wild, that's when Durbrain will set loose the pigeons! They're trained to poop on that stage, like they did earlier—only their *real* target is the headmaster!'

'We've got to stop Durbrain,' said Sara.

Sam paused. 'Maybe we could stop him just

after he's set them loose,' he suggested. 'It *would* be brilliantly funny!'

'You want to give Collier and Durbrain the satisfaction?'

He sighed. 'I guess not.'

'Then get yourself off to that stage,' said Sara. 'Keep the Head out of the way. I'm going to sort out Durbrain.' She nodded to herself as she marched to the door on her wobbly legs. 'He puts the "pig" into pigeon. And he is going to get what's coming to him . . .'

Sam ran like hell from the office and out of the block. Sara was right—no way could he let Collier enjoy any kind of a happy ending, not after what he and his little gang had done.

On his way to the playing fields he came across Memphis hovering nervously with a tearful Daisy. She must have retrieved the monk's costume from the bin; she was clutching it like a security blanket. A dazed Ferret was sitting on top of an equally dazed Pacemaker, pinning him to the ground. Sam skidded to a halt beside them.

'Everything all right?' he asked.

'I'm a teacher,' sighed Ferret.

Sam nodded sympathetically and looked at Memphis. 'Apart from that?'

'I don't know if the police believed me, but I guess the fire brigade's on its way. What happened?' she demanded. 'Did you find Sara?'

'She's fine,' he panted. 'And *nothing* happened. Looks like the whole thing was a joke.' He looked at Daisy. 'No building work required.'

Daisy looked baffled, perhaps unsure whether to be relieved or upset. 'But . . . he promised he would swing that work for my dad!'

'Yeah, well—what do you expect when you do deals with loopy old teachers?' Sam grabbed the habit from her. 'Might come in handy,' he explained. 'Anyway, I can't stop. I've got to stop the play. If the police show, tell them to come to the stage!'

'Where's Sara now?' asked Memphis.

'Up at the farm, dealing with Durbrain,' he called over his shoulder as he sped off for the playing fields. 'She's a girl on a mission. And so am I!' He paused, turned back round. 'That came out wrong, but you know what I mean.'

'Good luck!' Memphis shouted.

Sam ran off again. He hadn't done any exercise since running every race in the sports day a few weeks back—which had nearly killed him. But he tried to imagine himself as the queen's bodyguard, who'd uncovered a terrible plot. He had to keep the queen safe, at any cost.

Well, perhaps not *any* cost, he thought, slowing down as a stitch began to throb in his side.

No. He couldn't give up. Sam wiped his sweating forehead with the red robe and forced himself on.

The assembly was in sight. Hundreds of students sat cross-legged in the field, arranged in a giant rectangle, flanked on each side by a row of teachers. At the far end of the rectangle stood the stage, and Fido was at the front (looking *very* stupid in Sara's red cloak, just as she had predicted) shouting out his lines. From this distance he couldn't hear quite what was being said over the sound of the blood pounding through his ears. Something about wishing Killer a happy retirement or something . . .

Suddenly, to Sam's dismay, a huge round of applause started. Fido took a bow and his cast trooped back on to join him. The stage was awash with red figures, and Durbrain's red splodges on the scenery glowed in the sunshine like neon lights.

Sam pushed himself faster, gritting his teeth, tearing up the grass as he ran, and ran and ran . . .

Sara vaulted the gate to the school farm and pelted down the path. 'Durbrain!' she yelled. 'I've got a bone to pick with you—probably one of yours, once I've broken it!' She ran round the building, searching for him. At the back, on the grass, a number of large wicker hampers had been arranged. She could hear the cooing and jostling of birds inside. Either someone was planning a raw pigeon picnic or Durbrain was almost ready to rock.

'Durbrain!' she shouted again, staring all around. 'Come out and face me, girl to worm!'

Durbrain peered out from behind one of the oversized hampers. 'I'm not a girl!' he complained.

'I'll tell you what *you* are,' said Sara, advancing threateningly. 'You are in the deepest of very deep doo-doo.'

'Not me,' he smirked. 'That's the Head you're talking about. Gonna be up to his ears in the stuff!'

Suddenly, the sound of applause floated across from the playing fields. The crowd must have loved the play. The play she'd worked her butt off for. The play that was supposed to be sending her out of Freekham High on a high note.

Now she'd missed the whole thing. Thanks to this curly-haired, fat-headed, lumpy-browed, cheating, miserable little . . .

Durbrain actually squeaked with fear as she ran towards him. But then he flipped open the lid of the first basket, and a bunch of pigeons flew out, stopping her in her tracks as she tried to avoid them. He opened another basket—*more* birds flapped out. The air seemed thick with them. She ducked down and kept on towards him but couldn't stop him from opening a third basket, a fourth, a fifth . . .

He was about to unlatch the sixth when she lunged for it and threw herself on top of the lid, reaching out to grab him. But she was just a fraction too slow to stop him, and he ducked back.

While Sara righted herself, Durbrain produced

a little whistle from his pocket and started blowing strange, twittering toots. The pigeons above them—there had to be sixty, at least—stopped their random flapping and, to her amazement, organized themselves into a circular flight path. Durbrain tooted again and they set off together in the direction of the playing fields.

'Ha!' cried Durbrain. 'You see? Everyone thinks I'm thick. But I'm a genius!'

'You may be a genius at blowing a whistle,' shouted Sara. 'But the whistle's been blown on your mad little scheme. Sam will sort it.'

'We'll see about that!' yelled Durbrain, sprinting away up the length of the Farm Block building towards the path. 'Whatever, you'll never catch me now!'

But suddenly, someone stuck out a leg from behind the farm building and Durbrain tripped over it. He went flying through the air and fell face-first in a dazed heap.

The owner of the leg came into view—Memphis.

'Sam said you were headed here,' she explained. 'Thought maybe you could use a hand. Or a well-placed foot.'

'Memph, you're incredible!' Sara cheered, and dragged one of the empty baskets over to where Durbrain lay groaning. 'Now, let's pack him away for later.'

Between them, they lifted the lump and jammed him into the big basket. Sara secured the lid with its buckle, then gave Memphis a hug.

'I left Ferret in charge of Daisy and Pacemaker,' Memphis told her. 'He's almost back to his old self. Sam *did* tell you about—?'

Sara nodded quickly. 'Yeah, kind of. Come on, let's follow those pigeons. I was supposed to stop them, but I messed up,' she sighed. 'So now it's all down to Sam reaching the Head in time.'

'Great,' said Memphis, falling into step with Sara as she ran off. 'We have to rely on the most unpunctual boy in the school being on time for the first time in his life. Like that's going to happen.'

'Well, you never can tell, Memph,' said Sara, thinking back to the Head's office with a half-smile. 'Take it from me—that boy is full of surprises.'

* * *

186

Sam's chest felt as if it was bursting, his clothes were sodden with sweat, but he kept on running. *Please let Sara have stopped Durbrain in time*, he thought, again and again, harder and harder as if that could make it true. Then he could reach the stage, collapse safely and wait for an ambulance to airlift him away to a hospital for the critically puffed-out.

He glanced behind him. A dark circling band was whirling above the school like a sinister halo.

Pigeons.

So Sara hadn't been in time. His safety net had failed. It was all down to him.

Sam ran on. He passed what seemed to be an endless number of baffled teachers and surprised students, nearly whipping them as he went with the edges of his habit still clutched tightly in one hand. But finally he was nearing the stage. He could hear the Head now, speaking a little uncertainly as if he couldn't quite remember what he wanted to say. The old duffer kept touching his forehead absent-mindedly, as though he had a headache.

If he touched it in another minute or two he'd know all about it.

'Look out!' Sam tried to yell, but it came out as, 'Hrrrr hrrr'—he was too out of breath to even whisper, let alone shout. Fido, Flange, and the cast stared at him from the stage as he approached, all frowns and confusion. And Killer, sitting close by the stage with an umbrella handy, had seen him too. Sam saw the panic in the old boy's eyes and smiled grimly.

But the pigeons were approaching fast, speeding across the sky like dark lightning.

Ruth saw them first, in her red ape suit. 'Not again!' she shrieked.

'Incoming!' yelled Ashley.

The Head jumped as if he'd had an electric shock and turned round in bewilderment.

'Clear the stage!' Sam croaked, even as he staggered up on to it. But no one could hear him over the cast's ensemble screams.

What the hell, thought Sam. In for a penny, in for a pound.

As the pigeons swooped down, Sam rugby-tackled his headmaster and brought him crashing to the ground.

A massive, disbelieving gasp went up from every student and teacher present. For a moment, Sam thought maybe the sonic shock-wave had warded off the pigeons. Then he remembered the way they'd behaved back in period four. First, the sighting run—then the dropping of droppings.

Already the birds were falling into formation, ready to make the second pass.

'What is the meaning of this, Innocent?' spluttered the Head, struggling to free himself.

'Sorry, sir,' he gasped. 'Got to hide your face.' Sam rolled the headmaster over onto his tummy. Then he grabbed the nearest bits of cardboard scenery and dropped them over his head.

'Sam!' squawked Fido from the edge of the stage. 'You'll get expelled!'

'Just get that dumb cape off, Fido!' Sam yelled hoarsely. 'All of you, take off your red costumes! Knock down the back wall of the stage! Red is the trigger! The pigeons are trained to "see red" whenever they see red! *Go!*'

The cast started screaming and stripping and scattering. The pigeons were swooping down again, distracting the baffled assembly. Some teachers had set off towards the stage—Hayes and Penter with indecent enthusiasm—clearly ready to inflict some of the world's greatest teacher punishments on Sam.

But Killer Collier was far closer and keener. Possessed with a speed born of desperation, he bumbled onto the stage waving his umbrella like an offensive weapon. 'Stop it, Innocent!' he cried. 'Get back, boy! I shall not be cheated of my revenge!'

The pigeons were looming large and wobble-bottomed above the stage.

In desperation, Sam chucked his monk's habit over Collier. Again, the crowd gasped in horrified disbelief. With a muffled cry, Killer stopped dead, desperately pulling at the rich red cloth.

But Sam wasn't stopping there. He grabbed Fido's discarded cloak and draped that around Collier's neck. And the Mountie jacket that Ashley had shrugged off, that went over the old boy too. Then Sam threw himself off the stage into the front row of the audience for a soft landing.

And when the pigeons zoomed down—ready for the kill and seeing red—there was only one target.

Collier managed to tear his way free of the costumes—just as half a tonne of pigeons' bottom-sludge landed on his silvery head. With a rasping splutter of rage and dismay, he collapsed under the sheer, slimy weight of it.

'Noooooooooooo!' yelled Collier.

'*Yes*,' said Sam quietly from his front row seat, with more satisfaction than he had ever known in his entire life.

And as Collier sat there, floundering in pigeon muck, an almighty gale of laughter went up from the whole school, followed by a massive round of applause. Sam stood up and took a bow.

Just as Penter and Hayes took hold of him.

'You've pushed your luck too far this time, Innocent,' roared Penter.

'This goes down in the big book,' added Hayes, quietly but no less frightening.

'Wait a moment if you please, gentlemen.' The Head had thrown off his cardboard cover, taken in the full horror of Collier's predicament, and now held up a commanding hand. 'I'm not sure what's going on here, Innocent. Either your behaviour is that of a mad and rabid animal—

or of a spirited lad with good intentions. Which is it?'

Penter and Hayes watched him closely, like guard dogs awaiting the order to bite.

Sam opened his mouth to speak. But someone beat him to it.

'That boy is a *hero*!'

It was the booming voice of Mr Ferret. He was nearing the stage, marching the protesting Pacemaker ahead of him while dragging Daisy along behind him. 'He is!' Ferret declared in front of the whole school. 'He and his friends got caught up in a mad mystery of bombs, pigeons, kidnap, and revenge—and they've saved the day!'

'Gracious, Mr Ferret, where did you spring from?' The Head stared at him, baffled. 'I thought you were away on emergency leave!'

'I was away, and it was an emergency all right,' Ferret boomed. 'But I've spent since Wednesday locked up in the Humanities storeroom by Collier and his nutty major friend here!'

A collective gasp went up from the school. Sam was surprised that anything could still shock the students after all they had witnessed today.

Penter turned a funny colour and peered at Ferret in alarm. 'You been drinking, Roger?'

'Mungleberry juice!' he roared, shaking Pacemaker by the scruff of the neck. 'That's what I've been made to drink! Messed up my memory for a while—but not for long.'

'That can't be!' insisted Pacemaker. 'It *does* work; I've tested it on myself. And *I* can barely remember a thing!'

'That's because—with respect, sir—you're half-potty anyway,' said Collier sharply.

'Half-potty? Me?!' screeched Pacemaker. But then he stopped to consider. 'Yes, you may have a point.'

'Collier locked me up because I found him training pigeons in *my* lofts to do this to you, Head,' Ferret explained. 'He wanted to humiliate you in front of the whole school for forcing him into retirement!'

The Head frowned at Collier. 'I think you have some explaining to do, Lionel.'

'And if you're thinking of suggesting the Head's office for a chat, think again,' Sam added. 'I fixed the little surprise you and Dennis Durban arranged in there.'

Collier dipped his head, and sticky brown dribbles slopped off his chin. 'My little "bomb" has gone off?'

'Brrrr-rrrr-innnnng,' chimed Sam.

The old man shrugged, defeated. 'I notice my predicament is a little less messy than it could have been. Do I take it Durban was stopped before he could release all of the pigeons?'

'That's right!' panted Sara, she and Memphis running up to join Ferret and friends. 'And now he's back at the farm trussed up in one of those pigeon baskets.'

'See how *he* likes it,' added Memphis.

Then Daisy stepped forwards, glaring at Collier. 'You tricked me into getting involved in all this! You lied! You made me think you were really going to get my dad work by blowing up the Head's office!'

A growing wave of scandalized chat was spreading through students and teachers alike. Sam half-smiled. He and Sara may have missed the play—but that was nothing compared to the drama going on live and unscripted right now.

'I misled you a little, Daisy,' said Collier. 'But I meant what I said about work for your father.

My bungalow is built on a good-sized plot of land, and I've a tidy sum of money salted away. Since I will soon be in prison, no doubt, neither will be of any use to me. So I want your father to build a retirement home for me and some of my old soldier chummies. A place for me to stay, when I get out.'

Daisy gulped. 'You're not messing?'

'*Messy*, perhaps,' grumbled Collier. 'But I mean what I say.'

She turned to Sara and Memphis in disbelief, then grabbed them both in a clumsy embrace.

Sam turned back to Collier. 'You *knew* the mungleberry juice would never stop Mr Ferret and me telling the police what you'd done,' he realized. 'You *always* knew you'd get caught for this. And yet you still went ahead and did it. Why?'

'Because all these long years,' said Collier, 'I've dreaded the thought of having to retire. Giving up my job. Fading away, all alone, forgotten about.' He smiled, shuffled over to the edge of the stage and addressed the dazed crowd. 'Well, you won't forget me now, will you? You'll each remember me for as long as you live!'

In the distance, Sam could hear wailing sirens approaching. Police, fire engine, or ambulance? Didn't matter, he supposed—they could do with all three.

'Ha! Ha! And when the press get hold of my story, the whole country will know about me! I'll never be forgotten, and I'll never fade away!' Collier chortled. 'I'm famous! *In*famous!'

'Not to mention, stark barking bonkers,' Sam muttered.

'So you see, Head,' Ferret insisted, 'Sam Innocent, Sara Knot, and Memphis Ball are actually the heroes of the hour! They saved me from imprisonment, you from a slimy soaking in pigeon poo, and stopped you from receiving an extra-nasty practical joke.' He turned to the shell-shocked school population ranged out before him. 'They don't deserve any punishment— but a round of applause!'

And, much to Sam's delight, the school seemed to agree with him. Students and teachers alike launched into an almost deafening round of applause. Adding a bit of stereo, Fido and Flange led the cast and crew of the play back onto the stage to lend their own whoops and cheers to the effort. And once the Head joined in, even Penter and Hayes had to clap half-heartedly.

Sam nodded to Sara and Memphis and they jogged over to join him on the stage. Together they basked in the applause as the sound rose up through the summer afternoon, loud enough to drive all pigeons from the skies.

HOMETIME

Sara was still on a high. She had never been applauded before. She had never felt so totally accepted as she did at that moment, standing on the stage with her best friends.

Just in time for it all to end.

An old life was ending for Killer and Pacemaker, too. When the police had showed up, Sara, Sam, and Memphis all went with the Head and Ferret to give statements at the top of the school drive. The policeman she'd spoken to had been utterly astounded, his eyebrows nudging against his hairline by the time she'd told her tale.

Perhaps he was new around Freekham.

Sara decided she felt like an old hand here, despite only arriving a few weeks ago. And as she stood with Sam at the edge of the scrum of police and suspects, she could tell he felt the same way.

'Did you hear those coppers?' Memphis was grinning her head off as she came over from the huddle to join them. 'They just checked our statements against each other, and can't believe they actually match!'

'I overheard the Head saying Durbrain's going to be expelled,' said Sam, 'for inciting pigeons to expel all over *him*.'

'He'll probably get kicked out of his pigeon association too,' Sara reflected. 'For giving the sport a bad name.'

'Well, at least Ferret gets something out of all this,' said Sam. 'Pacemaker's pigeons must think of that new loft as home, now. Looking after them will help take his mind off the fact he's a teacher!'

Collier had insisted to both the Head and the officers in charge that he had forced Daisy to do his dirty work for him, against her wishes—it seemed that she might get off with just a temporary exclusion. And Pacemaker in turn insisted that Collier was entirely innocent—as commanding officer, he took full responsibility for all that had happened. Collier pointed out that they had both left the army more than fifty years ago, and

Pacemaker got very huffy, muttering about 'dratted head-scrambling mungleberries'.

Neither of the old men had made any pleas for the law to go easy on Durbrain. Right now the poodle-haired slacker was sitting in the back of a police car—and from the miserable look on his face, he'd preferred the pigeon basket.

The hometime hooter blared out at a near-deafening level, as if it knew this was the last chance it would get all summer. The policemen covered their ears.

'Perhaps we should resume this conversation at the police station,' the Head yelled over the noise. 'Nine hundred students will be passing here any minute.'

'Point taken, sir,' said the detective in charge. 'Boys! Let's move the golden oldies into the cars!'

Pacemaker kept a stiff upper lip and an even stiffer backbone as he was marched off rigidly to the nearest police car. Collier followed on, a big smile on his mucky bewhiskered face.

'He almost seems to be enjoying this,' Memphis marvelled.

'Got what he wanted, hasn't he?' Sam shook his head in grudging admiration. 'He's gone out in a blaze of glory.'

Sara nodded. 'And so have we.'

'No one knows you're leaving yet,' murmured Memphis. 'You going to tell them?' She looked up at the crowds already coming into view, spilling out of the playing fields. 'This could be your last chance.'

Sam and Sara looked at each other.

'Maybe it's better to just slip away,' said Sara.

'I mean, what can anyone say?' added Sam. '"Oh, sorry to hear we'll never see you again. Bye then"?'

'Something like that,' Memphis agreed. 'But they'll actually mean it.'

'Yes, well,' said Sara hesitantly, 'I don't know for absolute, true-life definite certain that I am going yet.'

'Me neither,' Sam agreed. 'I mean, it's ninety-nine point nine per cent likely that my dad's going to take this new job—'

'—and there's more chance of the school suddenly exploding than my mum saying no to hers,' Sara went on. 'But you know, there's still a chance . . .'

Sam nodded, cringing. 'Imagine how embarrassing it would be if we showed up next term after saying goodbye!'

'You might find people were actually glad to see you.' Memphis raised an eyebrow. 'Here's *someone* who is, anyway.'

Sara turned to find Ruthless Cook marching up to them, ahead of the rest of the class. There was this weird thing on the big girl's face. It was a smile.

Ruthless threw a burly arm round Sam. 'You were awesome on that stage, Innocent,' she said. 'I've always wanted to rugby-tackle the Head like that.'

Highly alarmed, Sam wriggled in her grip. 'Well, he's standing just over there, be my guest.'

'Shame you all missed the play,' she added.

'Ooooh, what a calamity,' said Sam theatrically. 'Who did my line, in the end?'

Ruth swelled with pride. 'I did.'

'Dressed as an ape?'

'Duh. As a *monk*-ey.'

'That *joke* was a calamity!' said Sara. 'One of Fido's, right?'

'Course.' She smiled again. 'Anyway—thing is, I'm having a party next week. You know, to celebrate the first and last day of the play.' She handed them some grubby pieces of paper. 'You're all invited. Even you, baldy. Even you, Knot. And even you—prat features.'

Sam half-smiled. 'I'm overwhelmed.'

'You've gotta come. The whole class is coming.' She curled her thick fingers into a fist. 'No excuses accepted. Anyway, it'll be a laugh. Like the play was.' She beamed. 'I reckon Fido should organize one every term!'

'Speak of the devil,' said Sam, as Fido joined them.

'Speak of the inspiring writer, director, narrator, and all-round god of the theatre, you mean.' Fido beamed at Ruth. 'See you next week, monk-ey girl,' he told her. 'Looking forward to it.'

'Laters,' called Ruth, as she headed off down the school drive.

'Now I've seen everything,' said Sam. 'Ruthless Cook behaving like something resembling a human being—and all because of some silly school play?'

'Kind of gives you hope for the future, doesn't it,' said Fido, slipping an arm round Sara. 'It's brought us all together.'

She trod on his toe and he jumped back with a shout. 'Not *that* close together it hasn't.'

'Anyway, it's good we're all going to meet up again at Ruth's party,' said Memphis. She gave Sara and Sam a knowing smile. 'Means we don't have to worry about saying any lingering goodbyes now.'

'That *is* good,' Fido agreed, 'because I have to split. I was videoing the play and want to check it out. Shame I didn't leave it running during *your* performance, Sam!' He slapped him on the back. 'See you, mate. Catch up with you soon, yeah? Maybe we can go to Ruth's party together. I'll call you.'

'Yeah,' Sam agreed. 'That'd be good.'

Fido winked at Sara. 'And *you* can always call *me*, day or night.'

'What, rude names, you mean?' Sara held up her hand and waved goodbye. 'See ya, then, Dorian.'

He blew her a kiss and jogged off down the drive.

Their classmates were coming fast and furious now, smiling or waving or giving thumbs up as they hurried past. All the people who had made these past few weeks so memorable. Ginger and her loopy sock puppet . . . Ashley with his thumb obsession . . . Smithy and his stunt falls . . . Vicki and the chic clique . . . Still the faces kept coming, enemies as well as friends. Carl Witlow, Connor Flint, Colin Cox . . . bullies and schemers and general losers. She might not miss them, but she would never forget them.

The crowds thinned out quite quickly, as the police were encouraging people not to dawdle. Sara, Sam, and Memphis were the exceptions, and were allowed to linger—presumably because they'd already seen all there was to see. They watched the teachers trundling over the speed humps in their clapped-out cars, escaping the students for six blissful weeks. And when the traffic had passed they stood watching the boxy, modern buildings, strangely still now in the strong sunshine.

'I felt I belonged here,' Sara said quietly.

'Me too,' said Sam.

'Cheer up, you two,' said Memphis. 'Like you said, there's a *chance* you'll be staying on. I mean, sure, maybe it is about as likely as the school spontaneously blowing up, but—'

She was silenced as an enormous explosion boomed out from the middle of the school. A fireball belched out into the blue sky. The police staggered back, and the Head and Ferret, who'd been talking to the detective in charge, jumped into each other's arms.

'That came from the Humanities Block!' gasped Ferret. 'Where I was locked up!'

'My school!' wailed the Head. 'My beautiful school!'

'Of course!' gasped Sam. 'Ferret had an oil lamp—we left it on the floor in there. And there were so many chemicals spilled on that floor. If one or two were flammable . . .'

'Whoomph!' Sara concluded, staring in disbelief.

Killer had unwound the window of his police car. 'Don't worry, old chap!' he shouted. 'The school was empty, no one could have been hurt.' He looked jubilant, even as a policeman tried to pull him away from the window. 'Besides, this means more work for Daisy's dad—and it makes me look more shocking than ever! I'll be on the BBC by nightfall, just you wait!'

Police radioed for the firefighters they had only just sent home. Then they turned their attention to Sara, Sam, and Memphis, shooing all three of them away to the bottom of the school drive. Sara could see the Head on his knees, Collier's defiant fist punching the air through the car window, Ferret scratching his head in bewilderment, and the orange flames lapping thirstily at the endless blue above.

'Will you look at that?' Memphis was staring at the scene, her sea-green eyes glittering with a kind of triumph. 'You two are *so* coming back in September. Don't you get it? The odds are beaten!' She beamed. 'Your parents aren't going anywhere. Sorry, but there's no escape for either of you. Freekham High is where you belong.'

Sam tore his eyes away from the blaze and looked into Sara's eyes. A slow smile was spreading over his face. 'She could be right.'

Sara nodded. She couldn't help smiling back.

With a sharp whistling noise, a large box of blackened metal came crashing down at their feet. Sara jumped back in alarm. It was the old lunch box. Somehow it had been propelled all this way by the extraordinary blast.

The lid creaked open on disintegrating hinges. While the sandwiches and apple had been incinerated, the flask remained surprisingly intact.

Sara glanced at Sam and Memphis. 'Think someone somewhere wants us to drink a toast?'

'A toast to us not *being* toast,' Sam suggested.

'No,' said Memphis. 'A toast to many happy returns.'

'That's mungleberry juice,' said Sara, remembering the sickly smell of it in the storeroom. 'Drink that and we'll forget we ever came here.'

'Then I know what we should do with it.' Sam carefully picked up the steaming flask and pulled off the lid. Then he poured the thick red juice on the ground beside the sign which warned the world that this was *Freekham High—A Progressive School.*

Sara watched it drain away into the earth with satisfaction. 'Should help the old place forget about all this for a while . . .'

'Till the loopiness starts again next September,' Sam agreed happily.

'And we'll see you then,' said Memphis, staring at the blazing school as the sound of fire engine sirens stole into the hushed summer breeze. 'Till next time, Freekham High.'

Steve Cole spent a happy childhood being loud
and aspiring to amuse. At school his teachers often
despaired of him—one of them went so far as
to ban him from her English lessons, which
enhanced his reputation no end.

Having grown up liking stories, he went to university
to read more of them. A few years later he started
writing them too. Steve has also worked as a
researcher for radio and an editor of books and
magazines for both children and adults.

He is the creator of *Astrosaurs*, *Cows in Action*,
The Slime Squad and many other books for children.
The Day of the Monster Pigeons is his fourth novel
for Oxford University Press.

LOOK OUT FOR . . .

Flying Thumbs?
What's *that* all about?

Sam and Sara just want to get through the
first day at their new school without sticking out
like sore thumbs. But when real thumbs, and fingers,
start appearing all over the place, they realize that
Freekham High is seriously weird.

For lunch in the canteen there's baked potato with
thumbs and finger custard—followed by . . .
the biggest vomit-fest ever!

Psychic Sock?
What's *that* all about?

Things at Freekham High have just taken
a turn for the freakier! Shy, quiet Ginger Mutton
is suddenly the girl everyone wants to be with.
Why? Because she's started to predict
the future ... with a sock!

When Sam gets caught in the middle of one of Ginger's
psychic blunders, he and Sara decide it's time to get to the
bottom of the footwear fortune-telling once and for all ...

Camera Carnage?
What's *that* all about?

As if life at Freekham High isn't weird enough, now
someone's trying to make it even weirder by filming lots
of fake and freakish accidents to send to a TV show.

Catching the school bully's gruesomely grotty grundies
on camera could be a dangerous move and when
one of the teachers takes a sudden interest in getting
hold of the evidence, Sam, Sara and their friends are
more determined than ever that it shouldn't fall
into the wrong hands.